POLLY

Graham Duncanson

Also by this author

Mating Lions
Fiona
Francesca
Anna
Katie
Emily

Abbreviations

ADVS.	Assistant Director of Veterinary Services
CBPP	Contagious Bovine Pleural Pneumonia
DC	District Commissioner
DLO	District Livestock Officer
DO	District Officer
DVS	Director of Veterinary Services
FAO	Food and Agricultural Organisation
FMD	Foot and Mouth Disease
LMD	Livestock Marketing Division
NFD	Northern Frontier District
ODA	Overseas Development Agency
PM	Post Mortem
PPL	Private Pilot's License
PC	Provincial Commissioner

Chapter 1

Polly loses her father

Polly's father had been her rock. She had never known her mother who had died, when she was born in the summer of 1945. Now he was dead having been gored to death by a buffalo. He had just managed to live long enough to grip her tiny hand in his fist and say,

"Goodbye Polly. Remember you are the very best. You are special."

He was a professional hunter. A client had wounded an old bull and he had gone into thick bush to finish it off. Instead it had finished him. Gideon his faithful gun bearer had killed the buffalo and got him back to camp. Using the camp radio, the Flying Doctor had been summoned. Thus he was in Nairobi Hospital, when Polly had flown in from School in the U.K.

Polly had been doing her six form years in Norwich at a day school called 'Norwich High School'. She stayed with her father's elder sister. She had just finished her last 'A' level paper, when she got called into the headmistress.

Miss Burrows ruled the school with a rod of iron. She only accepted excellence. Polly did not excel in the classroom, but she did excel on the running track and in the swimming pool. Miss Burrows admired her. She had also admired her father. Few ladies did not. Miss Burrows under her forbidding exterior had a kind streak. She was well aware of the importance of Hector Cavendish in Polly's life. Miss Burrows did not relish the task in hand, but she faced it with compassion and common sense.

She came across her office to greet Polly, and immediately put her arm around Polly's shoulder.

"I have dreadful news my dear. Your father has been attacked by a buffalo. He is fighting for his life in Nairobi Hospital. My secretary is trying to arrange a flight for you, as we speak." Miss Burrows had expected tears, instead Polly said,

"Thank you Miss Burrows. I will go to him immediately, as he will need me. Thank you for all you have done for my education. I would be grateful if your secretary could arrange to have all my personal affects sent out to Kenya. I will run to the station via my Aunt, to collect my passport and Yellow Fever Vaccination Certificate, together with some hand luggage.

She turned on her heel leaving a stunned Miss Burrows who watched her out of the window. She saw her run, totally against school regulations, to the school gates and turn left down The Newmarket Road.

Miss Clemenceau came into Miss Burrow's office saying,

"I have arranged a flight for Polly Cavendish. She flies on East African Airways tonight at 20.30 from Heathrow." Miss Burrows replied,

"Thank you Miss Clemenceau. She has already left. Can you ring the details to her Aunt, as she is going there to pick up her passport. It was most odd. She seemed to mature in front of my eyes. She left, thanking us, but with absolutely no regrets. She obviously could not wait to return to her beloved Kenya. I think if you had not arranged a flight, she would have run the whole way. She is a superb athlete. I just hope her intellect will be able to keep up." Miss Clemenceau replied,

"It is hardly my place to comment, but I think her intelligence has been deeply hidden. It may be related to having a very dominant father. She has a marvellous gift for languages. I think she will blossom like the grass in Kenya after the drought. I think she will not only be remembered here at the High School as the fastest girl to run a mile, but will achieve much more."

"Well I hope you are right. The news was not encouraging about her father."

Polly found her father's funeral a nightmare. She would have liked it to have been a quiet affair for the staff. Instead it became a circus. Her home was on a ranch on the Athi plains just outside the Nairobi flight zone. There was an airstrip. Friends flew in and parked their planes and then walked up to the house. They then, expected a drink and food. In fact those who weren't actually flying an airplane, expected several drinks.

2

Polly had organised the hunting staff to carry the coffin. She walked behind with Gideon beside her. All the rest of the African staff then followed. Some of the European friends were not pleased to be at the back. The very short service was conducted in Swahili on Polly's instructions. After she had thrown in the first handful of soil she walked with Gideon to a small knoll about a hundred yards from the grave. Lady Standup, her Godmother tried to walk with them. Polly turned to her,

"Auntie Margaret I would like to be alone with Gideon." Lady Standup was about to protest, but Polly's look did not brook an argument. Polly continued to talk to Gideon in his tribal language, as they walked away.

"You will have to be my father now Gideon."

"Miss. Polly, I can never replace your father. However I will be your servant and if you will allow it, your friend."

"I will value your friendship. I intend to continue the hunting operation, so that all the staff will continue to have employment."

"Who will be the hunter?"

"You will be, Gideon. I have always hated it, when clients called father a 'White Hunter'. He was a professional hunter. The colour of his skin was totally irrelevant."

"Miss. Polly, There will be a lot of prejudice. The clients won't like it. Your father was very charismatic. I'm just a gun bearer."

"You have the respect of all the hunting staff. Some clients will go to other hunters, but hopefully we will have enough to keep going. I will have to man up to support you with the hunting. A few clients will enjoy having a woman in the camp. I know in your eyes I'm only a young girl, but somehow overnight I have aged." She laughed then and added,

"If I was your wife, I would probably have three children by now and my tits would hang down to my waist." Gideon smiled,

"I'm glad we are speaking my language, if Lady Standup could hear you, she would have me beaten."

"You must not worry, Gideon. I'm not my father's daughter for nothing. I will control the likes of Lady Standup."

They continued standing together looking down at the mourners. When the last had turned towards the ranch, they walked behind.

3

Gideon left her at the house and she went in to face the babble of voices. Everyone wanted to say how sorry they were. Many offered her their help. Polly had no way of knowing which of these offers were kind and well meaning, or whether there was an element of self interest. She noticed that the men spent more time looking at her than they had done two years ago, when she had left to go to Norwich. A man came up to her and suddenly there was a hush in the room. It was as if everyone was holding their breath. He was tall with blond hair. He was good looking in a Nordic way. Polly immediately guessed he was the client that had wounded the buffalo. He introduced himself as Wolfgang. He then said,

"I'm truly sorry about your father. I would have gone into the thicket to put the animal out of its misery, but your father insisted that it was his job." Polly answered,

"Indeed it was. There are probably bad parts and good parts to every job. I'm too young to have experience, as I only left school three days ago. What is your job?" Wolfgang was surprised by her question.

"I do not have a job." Polly smiled,

"I don't envy you. I have been looking forward to working for as long as I can remember. Will you be returning to hunt with us?" Once again Wolfgang was surprised by the question.

"I had not thought that you would be continuing to hunt."

The whole room was silent now.

"Oh yes we will be continuing, not least because it is what my father would have wanted. I'm sure small things will change, hopefully for the better with a women's touch, but the operation will carry on. I think we still have to find you a leopard. If you are agreeable I will get things organised tomorrow. I'm sure you understand that all the staff wanted to attend the funeral."

Wolfgang hesitated. He had little hunting experience. He had been happy with Hector Cavendish by his side, but his courage had deserted him, when the buffalo had charged. He had shot too early and he knew that he could not have followed up the bull. It had been bravado which had made him volunteer. Always before in his life, his father's money had solved everything. It would have to save the day. He replied,

4

"I will leave the leopard. I would not want to hunt without your father. However I will remit double the fee to your father's company."

Polly held out her hand,

"That is extremely generous. As a little girl I had a much loved cat, so I do not enjoy hunting lion or leopard. I was not looking forward to hunting a leopard. I have only shot one leopard and I was sad afterwards. I suppose that was rather an immature failing. I hope it was immaturity. I am two years older now."

They shook hands and as Wolfgang was about to turn, he had an idea.

"I have a young nephew who has always wanted to hunt would you take him to hunt my leopard?"

Polly replied with a cheeky smile,

"Certainly we will take him, but only if he is as good looking as you?" Polly's charm had one Wolfgang over.

When she was lying in bed that night, sleep eluded her. Emotionally she was totally drained. She reflected on her behaviour at the funeral. *'Why had she not wept? Why had she wanted to be alone with Gideon? She knew there would be gossip between the old Kenyan matrons. Why had she made it worse?'* At last sleep claimed her. She slept well and was only awakened by Josiah, bringing in her tea. The sun had been up for over an hour. He obviously thought it was time for the new mistress of the house to attend to her duties. The new mistress took time to drink her tea and plan her day, before quickly dressing and eating a hearty breakfast. She complimented Josiah on the excellent fry-up, and said that he would soon make her fat. He went to the kitchen chuckling. Polly was not sure whether that was because, he thought she was too thin, or whether he thought young nubile girls should be well covered and have big bottoms. Polly was determined she was going to stay slim, and certainly she did not want a big bottom!

She knew that Gideon would have the hunting team organised. Wolfgang had said his nephew would arrive in three days, so the main priority was to find a leopard. Luckily her neighbour Ed Truscott, an old rancher, had said he was having trouble with a leopard taking his sheep, so Gideon did not have to cast too wide a net.

Polly knew her first duty was to go and see Alan White, her father's solicitor. He had said yesterday that he would be pleased to see her at 10.00 am. Roly Brown, the bank manager, had also asked her to call in the morning. Polly was about to go into Nairobi dressed as she was in shorts and a top, but then she decided to change. She knew that the last impression she wanted to make was, as an immature young girl. She smiled at herself in the mirror. Miss Burrows would have been proud of her. She got Noah, her father's driver to drive her. There was going to be no running today. She had run out of Miss Burrow's office, when she had left school, just to give the whole place two fingers. Now she was free, she was happy to choose to be demure.

Noah parked in front of the solicitor's office. Poly thanked him and made him laugh by saying that she had hitched up her skirt to get out of the rather high Landrover, as her skirt was a bit tight, not because she was on the lookout for a husband!

Alan White was totally predictable. He read the very short simple will to her which made her the sole beneficiary, other than a list of money for all the staff. Finally he read out her father's last bit of advice. 'Polly, you have the most beautiful smile. Use it. It will get you much further than a frown'. Polly could not stop herself. She burst into tears. She let Alan put his arm around her. Then she blew her nose, dried her eyes and smiled at him. Alan said,

"Forgive my presumption, but I agree with your late father. You have the most beautiful smile. May I kiss your hand and pretend I am forty years younger?" Polly laughed,

"I would like that. I don't care how old you are. You are very good looking man."

Alan beamed with pleasure.

Sadly there were no smiles from Roly Brown at 'Standard Bank'. Polly had no idea what was likely to happen, when she was ushered into his enormous office with its very imposing desk. He was by Kenyan standards a 'high flier' He was not yet forty and was the manager of the Nairobi branch which was the biggest in the country. He offered her a seat with a wave of the hand, as the office boy closed the door.

"Young lady, you should have consulted with me before you made such a bold commitment yesterday at your father's funeral. I cannot allow your father's enterprise to continue. The bank will fore close on your father's estate before the end of the week. It would not have been seemly for us to have done anything, until after the funeral."

Poly had a vision of her father, when he hugged her, when he had left her at 'Norwich High School' two years ago. She remembered being slightly perplexed, when he had said,

"I have paid the two years of fees in advance, just in case there are problems getting money out of Kenya." She had not thought anything more about it. Now she had a very dreadful feeling in her stomach. However she remembered her father's last piece of advice. She smiled and said,

"May I call you Roly? Then you can call me Polly, rather than young lady which is very formal."

This caught him by surprise. He suddenly had a vision of her on his arm walking into the Muthaiga Club' Ball. He stuttered and replied,

"Of course." Poly continued to smile and said,

"Perhaps you would like to take me through the figures? I do not suffer from discalculia!" He stuttered again,

"Of course." Poly wondered if that was his standard reply to everything.

Then there was a silence. Polly gave him her most dazzling smile and said,

"You were going to explain the figures to me." Roly thought, *'what is it about this girl who is half my age and seems to totally control any conversation.'*

"Of course. Yes I was." Polly thought, *'I think I will strangle him if he says, 'of course' again.*

"When I first joined the bank, your father borrowed money from us, when he started taking clients hunting. I arranged the loan for him. He mortgaged the house and the small amount of surrounding land. His wealthy neighbours owned all the large areas of land in the vicinity. In those days professional hunting was a precarious occupation. Not only was it dangerous, but also any profit depended to a large extent on the personal charisma of the hunter. Your father was an excellent hunter, but he was not a good businessman. His debts continually mounted. Two years ago he had a dreadful year

7

and we nearly called in his loan. He came to see me and we allowed him to carry on. Sadly now he has been killed and the bank will need to be paid." Polly replied,

"Surely Wolfgang's offer to give me double his fee will help?"

"That would sadly only cover the interest on the loan for six months. We need assets to be sold to lessen the debt. You have no assets, and no charisma to keep money coming in." Much to his surprise, Polly laughed,

"Well Roly. I will have to take your advice. I will have to sell my body. It is the only asset I have. I'm sure there were some wealthy men who flew in yesterday who might take you up, if you offer them my body. It is in the interest of your bank to raise the funds, as I suspect that any others assets will not realise enough money. Poor Dad is no longer here to offer you his charisma; you will have to work something out with his daughter. I will need a couple of weeks to allow Wolfgang's nephew to kill his leopard and then I will come and see you. I will leave you to draw up a business plan. I'm sure you have inside information. It would be very foolish of me to give myself to some man who appears to be wealthy, but actually already owes you a hat full of money. See you in two weeks."

Polly left him opening and shutting his mouth, like a goldfish. She thought, '*At least he didn't say of course.*'

Chapter 2

Polly becomes a business woman

Polly realised how naïve she had been. Her first job on her return home was to look in her father's safe and in his filing cabinet. He might not have been a good businessman, but he had not been a fool. In the safe she found quite a large amount of cash, not only in Kenyan shillings, but also in foreign currency. She had enough Kenyan currency to pay the staff for about three months. She would have to change the foreign currency to keep the operation running. However she had enough sense to know that the longer she could keep the foreign currency the better. With independence the value of the Kenyan shilling was bound to drop. She also found some jewellery which she assumed must have been her mother's. It was in a separate strong box in the safe. It gave her an idea. She put all the foreign currency in the same box and took it into the bank the next morning. She said to an under manager that it was her mother's jewellery and so she wanted it held in the bank for safe keeping. She was given a receipt for the strong box. She knew that Roly would hear about it which was all to the good. She did not want all that money in the house. Obviously she did not want Roly to know about the cash.

Wolfgang's nephew, called Max arrived on schedule. Polly thought he was very cocky for a seventeen year old boy. However, having been at an all girls' school, she realised that she knew very little about adolescent boys. She knew if Max was typical she was going to keep very well clear of them! However Polly was very clever at hiding her feelings.

She and Gideon spent two days with him trying to teach him, how to shoot and more importantly how to be safe. Polly was concerned that because he was so arrogant, he did not really listen. She could understand that he did not want to take instruction from a mere girl, but it infuriated her that he had so little respect for Gideon and the rest of the staff.

Word came in from the trackers that they had sighted the leopard. It was a big old male, slightly lame on its left hind leg. It would be a good trophy. Early the next morning Gideon had checked out his hiding place. It was on a small kopje. The leopard had chosen well, as surrounding the kopje was thick bush, so he had several ways of escape. Gideon said to Polly that he was not happy. However he thought that they probably would not get the leopard in any better position. He would be cunning and if he was not so strong on a hind leg, he would not be able to take his kill up into a tree.

They gave Max a final briefing in the afternoon. Gideon stressed how it was vital that Max took his time and did not shoot too early. Gideon said it was much better not to shoot than to place a poor shot. Before dark they took up their position in the make-shift hide. Gideon was close to Max, but just slightly behind him and to his left, as Max was shooting off his right shoulder.

Polly's task was to be, to the side of them both, with the big heavy torch on its sturdy tripod. When Gideon touched her shoulder she was to turn on the torch. They only planned to use the lamp if there was any danger to Max. Both Max and Gideon had double barrelled 30.06 rifles. Polly brought her trusted 12 bore shot gun with special cartridges for killing large cats called SSG. Then they had to wait.

It was not dark, when they heard the crunching of bone and could see the leopard. They had not heard him arrive. The leopard made a majestic sight. Max fired. He missed the killing shot and must have hit too high up on the leopard's shoulder. The leopard turned giving him a good heart shot, but he was too slow and hit the leopard in the hips. This must have infuriated the leopard, as it turned back and charged. Max panicked, turned and ran away, knocking Gideon over. The leopard was almost on Gideon, when Polly took a step forward and fired both barrels of her shot gun. The ball bearings do not actually spread out, like normal shot from a shotgun, when used to kill game birds. They go into the animal through a hole that is only a little bigger than the bore of the gun. At that range they caused massive damage to the leopard's heart and lungs. Her shots killed the leopard instantly. However its momentum carried it on and, then it hit her, knocking her over on to Gideon. She landed in his celiac plexus winding him. She grabbed his gun, but did not need it, as the leopard was definitely dead. She helped him to his feet and put his head between his knees to get him breathing normally again.

"Thank you Miss Polly. You saved my life." Polly laughed,

"I will forgive you Mr Gideon, but remember in future I am just POLLY. I wonder where Max has run to. I imagine all the five miles home! We won't mention anything to anyone else. We will let him think he killed his leopard."

They scuffed the tracks so that the skinners would not be able to work out exactly what had happened. They would know that it had been SSG which had actually killed the animal, but they would be told by Gideon that Polly had finished it off.

When they got to the yard, the skinners were dispatched in a Landrover. Polly went into the big house, having said goodnight to Gideon. Josiah told her the guest had run in, close to exhaustion, and had gone to his room. Josiah gave her a cup of tea and Polly went into Max's room. She knew he was awake by the sound of his breathing. She said,

"Well done Max. You shot your Leopard. The skinners have gone out now. It should be a good trophy. I think your Uncle will be pleased.

"Please don't tell him I ran away."

"Nothing will be said by either Gideon or me. I can assure you. Gideon has a family, so if you can be generous with your tip, I would be grateful."

Then he wept. Polly put her arm around him, as she sat beside him. She thought, *Really he is just a little boy trying to be a man. Whatever am I? I am just a little girl trying to be a woman. I will have to hope I will be successful. I think all the staff depend on me. There is so much unemployment, I very much doubt if many of them would get jobs. It would do Max good to work, but I expect he will just be a playboy like his Uncle. I have got a lot to thank 'Norwich High School' for, not the least giving me a work ethic. I hope that's what Dad wanted'.*

Max was very subdued at breakfast. Polly did her best to cheer him up. She was not surprised, when he said he never wanted to go hunting again. He also let on that he did not think his Uncle would want to hunt again. He asked Polly if he could be driven into Nairobi. Apparently his Uncle was staying with the German

11

Ambassador. Polly soon organised Noah to take him. She was very surprised, when Max hugged her, when he came to leave.

Polly reflected that human nature was strange. Max had no idea that she did not like him and had absolutely no affection for him. She decided to discuss the whole potential disaster with Gideon, so that they might learn by it.

Gideon's only comment was,

"You hide your feelings very well. Your father used to do the same. I'm sure he would be proud of you."

As they did not have another client for six weeks, they decided to offer their services, as lion controllers to the local ranchers who were daily having cattle taken by lion. There were just too many lion in the area and the Game Department did not have the resources to control them. They both felt that hunting together would be good training. It would also keep the staff busy. They could make money in two ways; not only by charging the rancher for a successful kill, but also by selling the skin. Lion trophies commanded a good price on the American market.

They were very successful, but this led to problems with Lady Standup who heard what they were doing. She arrived at lunchtime, unannounced. Polly was eating alone on the veranda. Polly immediately offered her lunch which she accepted with rather poor grace. She then berated Polly. Polly was hurt and very cross, but she managed to hide her emotions. What really annoyed Polly was that the whole rant was carried out in front of Josiah. Eventually Lady Standup demanded,

"This behaviour has got to stop. You are getting a very bad reputation." Polly had reached her limit. Her hands were tied, as the last thing she wanted was for Lady Standup to know that she was about to go bankrupt. She rounded on Lady Standup,

"Auntie Margaret you are welcome to come at anytime to my house. However I would like you to observe some good manners and not treat me like an adolescent. I am endeavouring to continue to run a complex operation in my father's memory. If I was out partying every night I would accept criticism, however I'm working. I suggest you visit my neighbours and see what they think. They all seem to be grateful. Now can I offer you a coffee?"

12

Polly was somewhat amazed, as her Aunt seemed to deflate like a balloon. Her hand shook, when she was sipping her coffee. Polly was grateful to Josiah, as he had brought out the best china rather than a mug which is what Polly normally used. Polly got up and came and put her arm around her Aunt.

"What is really worrying you Auntie Margaret? I'm really only an insignificant eighteen year old girl!"

Her Aunt sniffed,

"I'm worried that you are getting too close to your staff. You should spend more time with Europeans." Polly smiled,

"Why don't you ask me to a dinner party? Father spent a fortune on my education."

"I was worried that you would bring that chap Gideon with you. You seemed very close at the funeral."

Polly could see it all now. Her Aunt was a racist which annoyed Polly. However Polly was well aware that the majority of Kenyans of that generation were racists. Polly's views were never going to change her Aunt. Somehow she was going to have to steer a very careful path. She said,

"Auntie Margaret, I'm sure you don't mind me reminding you that I am from a very different generation to you. That does not stop me acknowledging your views. I'm a loner and I am not really close to anyone. My father was my rock. He is no longer there for me. I will just come alone to any dinner party. I just beg you not to try and pair me off with any spare man, however suitable you might think he is. Equally I do not want you to think I'm gay!"

"Whatever do you mean, Polly?" Polly despaired,

"I mean Auntie Margaret that I am a totally normal heterosexual girl. I am not a homosexual. Gay means a lesbian."

"Oh I understand. I am sorry I am not very worldly, I'm afraid."

Polly was relieved that was the end of the conversation. She agreed to come to dinner in two night's time. She knew that would be a trial. However she knew that the following morning, when she had to go and meet Roly in the Standard Bank would be worse.

She dressed smartly. She joked with Josiah about it, as he had prepared a particularly good breakfast for her. She had on a full, mid-calf, floral, dress, so she had a joke with Noah about not catching a husband, as she got out of the Landrover. She was shown

13

into Roly's office as before. However his manner was subtly different. Polly picked up on it immediately. He was almost proud of the figures and financial plan that he had prepared. He came around his desk so that he could stand beside her and show them to her. He stood just a little too close. Polly instinctively went to move away, but she managed to stop herself. She realised, '*He fancies me. He wants my body. He does not want it sold to a wealthy rancher.*' She leant ever-so slightly towards him. His plan was hard, but with the cash she had, which he was unaware of, it was possible. She asked him, if she should sell her mother's jewellery. He had obviously heard about the strong-box. He advised against their sale, as he said with the value of the Kenyan Shilling dropping, they were a very worthwhile investment.

Polly then had an idea. She told him about hunting lion for her neighbours and the problems she had with her Aunt, Lady Standup. Then she took a gamble and said,

"If only I could get someone suitable to ask me to the 'Muthaiga Ball'?"

Polly had baited her hook. Would Roly take the bait? She held her breath, but breathed out very slowly, when he said,

"Would you partner me? I have some friends who are making up a table."

"Roly that would be really kind. I will try not to embarrass you too much. At least we will not have to talk about any banking or business problems."

So it was arranged for a week on Saturday. Roly's business plan was agreed without further discussion.

Auntie Margaret's diner party was not as bad as Polly had imagined. All the other guests were Auntie Margaret's friends who were not all her age, but obviously had similar views. Certain topics were forbidden items of conversation. Talking about, ranching, game poaching and the lack of rain was totally acceptable, so Polly could politely listen and add the odd comment or anecdote, when it was appropriate.

Polly was so thankful to Roly for his invitation. The 'Muthaiga Ball' came up in conversation. Polly casually mentioned that she was going on a table that included Roly. Apparently senior bank managers were acceptable. The fact that there was a wide gap in age did not seem to be a problem. So when Polly said good bye to her Aunt, she was relieved that Aunt Margaret said,

"I'm sorry I behaved so badly at your house the other day." Polly answered,

"Don't worry about it. I knew I would get a large amount of criticism from many quarters, when I decided to continue Father's business. Thank you for supper. I will look forward to seeing you at Muthaiga."

Polly was glad to get to her bed that night. It had been an ordeal, but not as bad as she had anticipated. She was dreading the 'Ball', but still she slept well.

Chapter 3

Muthaiga Ball

After a good breakfast she was ready to face the day. She sat in her father's office with Gideon and they did some serious planning. Their first clients were arriving in six days time on the Monday after the Saturday night at Muthaiga. They were Americans. They were a father and daughter. Polly did not know the age of the daughter; named Chloe, but father named Ret described himself as a fit sixty year-old. He wanted to shoot, 'The Big Five'. Polly had booked a big hunting block in Garissa District. She and Gideon knew of a good spot for a base camp in the dry country about ten miles north of the Tana River. It was a very dry area and so mosquitoes would not be a problem. The main difficulty would be water. They had a bowser and so they would have to bring water from the Tana River almost on a daily basis. Even if they could have put up with the mosquitoes they were not allowed nearer to the Tana River, as that was part of the Coast Province. Their hunting block was in North Eastern Province.

Polly had decided not to hire extra staff, to save money, but instead use some of the home staff and pay them extra as 'safari bonuses'. It would leave the ranch rather depleted, but every saving was important.

She was going to have to be very careful with Roly. She could not afford to upset him. Equally she did not like the idea of letting him get too close. She did not find him totally repulsive which was merciful. She did not mind the thought of him putting his arm around her or dancing fairly close, but she hoped she could get away with a peck on the cheek, when she said good night. She had a very good excuse that she had to get home, as he knew she had her clients arriving on Monday morning. Polly had no worries about driving herself. She certainly did not want him driving all the way out to the ranch, nor did she want Noah waiting up all night for her. She knew that the affair was likely to go on until dawn.

Polly was grateful to Roly that he was on time and was waiting for her on the lawn, where they got their free arrival champagne. Polly was pleased with her appearance. Her full-length evening dress was quite low-cut and sexy, but it had good wide shoulder-straps. Polly hated strapless ball gowns. She used to laugh when she saw other girls spending the whole night hitching up their fronts! The dress hugged her petite bottom and then flared out at her knees in a nineteen twenties style.

Roly obviously thought she looked good, as he could not take his eyes off her. The other men in the party were rather stuffy and were Roly's age group. Their wives were also in their late thirties so they were, either very condescending to Polly, treating her like a child, or were slightly bitchy, if they thought their husbands were paying too much attention to her.

Polly was very gregarious and had no problems chatting to strangers. She enjoyed her champagne, but was careful not to drink too much on an empty stomach. There was one girl in her mid thirties who seemed to be on her own. Polly saw she did not have an engagement or wedding ring. Her name was Ophelia Balls. When she was introduced, Polly had great difficulty in keeping a straight face. Polly learnt that she was on a blind date with a vet called Dick Brendon. Polly remembered Dick, from ten years ago. Her father had been away hunting. Dick had been really kind to her, when he had to destroy, her very elderly, first pony called, Jim. Jim had a twist of his large intestine. He was in a lot of pain. Dick had let her stand next to him, when he had shot Jim. Dick was a big man and had wrapped her in his arms. She had sobbed her heart out with her face in his shirt. It had been about ten 'o'clock at night. Instead of leaving her with the staff, he had taken her on another call to a calving cow. Polly had really enjoyed helping. She had loved feeling inside the cow and then feeling the calf's legs kicking. She and Dick had got very messy, but Polly was so grateful to him, as she would have had to try to go to sleep all alone at the ranch, having just seen Jim's body being dragged away. As it was she had gone to sleep in Dick's car. He had taken her home and put her into her bed, filthy dirty. He had then gone to sleep in a big arm chair next to her bed which her father used to sit in, when he read her a night-time story.

Dick was still there, when she woke at her normal time of 7 am. Josiah had come in to her room with her milky drink. Polly had then gone with Josiah and brought Dick a 'wake up' cup of tea. Still in their filthy clothes they had had breakfast together, before Dick had to go to work. She had thought he was marvellous. She wondered what she would think of him now.

Dick's blind date was not at all happy that Dick had not arrived by the time that they had to go to their table for supper. Polly sat next to her and tried in vain to cheer her up. When they all had finished the meal and were drinking their coffees, Dick arrived full of apologies, saying he had been called to do a caesarean on a cow and had tried to be as quick as he could. Polly went to organise the waiters to bring him some food, as she suspected that he was starving. Ophelia hardly bothered to say hello to him. Introductions were made by David Parsons who had organised the table. David introduced Polly, when she returned. To her surprise Dick recognised her. He opened his arms to her saying,

"I was so sorry to hear about your father, I heard about it, when I came home from overseas leave."

The loss of her father suddenly hit Polly. She burst into tears and went into his arms like she had done ten years earlier. She felt him stroking her hair with one hand and the other holding her very tightly to his body. She could not stop herself. She sobbed. She had bottled up all this emotion and this lovely kind man had allowed her to let go. He had not fully buttoned up his shirt. She had pressed her face against his chest. She was sure he smelt the same as he had done so long ago. No one could see, but she kissed his hairy chest. She wanted to stay like that forever. She heard him saying,

"Polly you have got me crying now. I managed not to cry, when I shot Jim, as I thought it would frighten you as a young girl seeing a man crying. I'm not so manly now. In fact I'm a bit of a softy."

Polly looked up at him and smiled,

"At least you don't have to worry about your makeup. You eat your food which has arrived. I will go and repair the damage." She walked quickly away to the ladies'.

Ophelia snapped,

"What was all that about? Is she your girl friend?" Dick laughed,

18

"She is only a girl friend in my dreams. I haven't seen her for ten years. She helped me do a calving, after I shot her first pony. She was a stunning little girl, aged eight, extremely tough and bright. She is a very beautiful woman now. I'm sure Hector, her father, would be very proud of her. Now Ophelia, once again let me say how sorry I am for being so late, but I will try and look after you properly. What do you do in Nairobi?"

Ophelia was only slightly mollified,

"I'm out from the UK on a long holiday. I'm a PA in London." Dick smiled,

"That sounds very important. You have picked a beautiful country to come to. Have you been on safari yet?"

"No, but I am hoping to find someone to take me?"

At that moment Polly returned, Dick teased her,

"You have repaired your war paint. What about my shirt?" His dress shirt was covered in lipstick. He had felt her little kiss on his chest. He had done his shirt buttons up. Somehow he did not want anyone to see she had kissed his chest. He had heard that she had been very brave at the funeral. He was not arrogant. He might think she was drop-dead gorgeous, but he certainly did not think she fancied him. He thought that being fifteen years her senior; he was a father like figure from the past. Poly smiled at him,

"Knowing you, Dick, it will go in the wash with the drapes from tonight's caesarean! Did you get a live calf?"

"Sadly I didn't. It was a schistosoma calf. I would have to have destroyed it anyway." Polly replied,

"I remember you telling me about those. You said they were sort of born inside out. I imagine them like a Bilharzia worm. The female Bilharzia worm keeps the male worm securely wrapped in her body until he has mated her. Then she eats him." She turned to Ophelia and said,

"Is there a guy here tonight which you would like to wrap yourself around and then eat?"

Ophelia was speechless and Dick was grinning from ear to ear. He said,

"Ophelia, would you like to dance. I'm afraid I'm not very tasty. Hopefully you have had a good supper!" He led her to the dance floor.

Polly was very correct. She had several dances with Roly and had one dance with all the other men on their table. Dick teased her, when they came to dance,

"I see I am allowed one dance. I'm glad it's a slow smouchy one." Polly moved her pelvis close to his, very provocatively, whispering,

"Don't get any big ideas, but I don't think your partner will live up to her name tonight."

"You are dead right. She is out to find a wealthy husband. I certainly don't fit the bill. You had better be careful. I think Roly has the hots for you."

"I know. I have not told anyone else, but I'm struggling financially. So far he has been very helpful. I will just have to keep him at arm's length. I'm sorry that I broke down, when you hugged me."

"Come and see me anytime, if you feel down. You can pretend to be a Bilharzia worm. I can't think of a more enjoyable way to die than to be eaten by you!"

"Richard Brendon. That was most inappropriate!"

"You started it."

"I suppose I did. Somehow I feel we are kindred spirits. I will remember your offer. You must also remember I would love to see you anytime at my house."

The danced finished and they returned to the table. Polly would have liked to have spent more time with Dick, but she knew she had to be a dutiful date. She took Roly over to Auntie Margaret's table. Auntie Margaret was delighted. Polly guessed that Roly was pleased, as it allowed him to be introduced to the others on her table who were bound to be influential.

Obviously the party was destined to go on until dawn, but Polly managed to give Roly a peck on the cheek, thank him for the evening and slip away to her Landrover. She was pleased to be cuddled up in bed before 3.00 am.

Polly had a long lie in the next morning. Josiah had sympathy for her. Polly knew that all the staff talked. They would know that she had come in alone in the early hours. Noah would have been grateful to her, for not making him wait at Muthaiga.

On Monday morning she went with Noah to meet Ret and Chloe at Embakasi. They had flown from the States via London, where they had had a five day stop over. They, therefore, had got over any jetlag. They had flown first class and had a mass of luggage. Polly had liked Ret immediately, as he had given Noah a hand to get the luggage into the Landrover. Polly had joked in their language with the guys hanging about, hoping to get tips, telling them she was a strong Kenyan girl. She told them that they were men. It was the women in Kenya who did the work. They all laughed, as they knew that was true, back in their Kikuyu tribal areas. Chloe had been listening. She asked,

"I have been trying to learn some Swahili; however I could not understand a word!" Polly laughed,

"Sorry that was Kikuyu. It is their tribal language. I will be pleased to help you learn Swahili. Africans are marvellous linguists. Very few visitors bother to try to learn proper Swahili." Chloe replied,

"That would be awesome if you could help me. I am not interested in hunting, but I want to learn about their culture."

Polly put Chloe at about forty. She was a statuesque brunette. Polly noticed she did not have a wedding ring or any evidence that she had ever worn one.

Polly got Ret to sit in front of the Landrover next to Noah. She sat in the second row of seats with Chloe. During the short ten mile drive to the 'Norfolk Hotel' in Nairobi, she pointed things out to them, as she knew they had never been to Kenya before. Ret said,

"We were sorry to hear about your father." Polly replied,

"I'm honoured that you have kept your booking. I will try to do my utmost to give you a good safari. Obviously I want to keep the business going in my father's memory. However what is very important to me is to continue to give employment to all the loyal staff. They have been so kind to me over the years. I will be quite open with you. The business is a real worry to me. It is very tempting to give it all up, and go and live in a flat in Nairobi, but that, neither fits with my upbringing, nor with my inclination." Chloe asked,

"How old are you?"

"I'm eighteen. I left school in the UK as soon as I heard that Father had been fatally injured. I only arrived just in time to say goodbye."

"I don't want to pry, but won't your Mother give you some help."

"Sadly, Mother died giving birth to me. I'm sure my Father was not celibate all those years, but there has never been another woman in the house. Father spared me a stepmother!" Chloe looked thoughtful and said,

"You are a marvellous girl. My heart goes out to you. I'm sure Father and I will have an excellent safari."

No more was said. Polly helped to check them into the 'Norfolk Hotel'. She made arrangements for the next morning.

Gideon had taken all the crew up to Garissa on Saturday. Polly was confident that the camp would be well set up by now. She had spoken to him on the Long Wave Radio, before she had left for the airport. He had reported that all was well. All Polly had to do was to get Ret and Chloe safely up to the camp. Hopefully they would leave some of their luggage at the 'Norfolk Hotel', as Polly had to take up some fresh food in cold boxes which was always bulky. She also had to take a table and chairs, so that they would be comfortable having lunch.

They set off in good time in the morning. They stopped on the road side near Thika at 'Delmonte' to buy some pineapples. Chloe looked on with interest, as Polly bartered with the group of Kikuyus. There was a lot of laughter. Obviously a European girl who spoke their language was unusual. Polly offered to stop at the 'Blue Posts Hotel' at Thika for coffee, but was glad that her clients were happy to push on, as they all knew they had a long hot drive, of over 250 miles, ahead of them on dirt roads. She pointed out some of the landmarks to them, like the Yatta Plateau. As Chloe seemed interested, she named some of the birds that they saw. They managed to reach a pleasant sandy spot, a mile off the road, past Mwingi which Noah knew for lunch. There were some big trees that gave them some welcome shade.

The lunch was excellent. Polly was pleased that Ret and Chloe had a 'Tusker' each. She had been worried that they might have wanted more exotic drinks. Also she was pleased, as they seemed happy for Noah to sit with them for lunch. They both had quite long naps in the Landrover in the afternoon. They crossed the bridge over the 'Tana River' in Garissa at 4.00pm and drove into the camp just before 5.00pm. Gideon was there to greet them. Josiah had tea and cake ready, as they collapsed in some camp chairs in the shade. They all were happy to rest and not been jolted about anymore by the corrugations on the road.

After tea Polly showed them to their tents. These had showers, basins and long-drops en suite. They agreed to meet in the mess tent for an early supper. It was a happy meal. Gideon told Ret that he had selected a good big bull buffalo for them to follow in the morning. Chloe asked if Polly would mind taking her on a game walk, as she actually did not like the idea of the hunting. She was happy for her Father, as this was something he had always wanted to do, but she said she would rather have a good walk and may be take some photos. Polly was entirely relaxed about this. She was so relieved that Gideon had been accepted as the professional hunter.

The men left about an hour before dawn, but Chloe and Polly had longer in bed and only set off after a cup of coffee, as the sun came up. Polly made sure they had an Ndorobo tracker, called Hak armed with a spear to guide them. She took a couple of water bottles, a compass and her shot gun. She was pleased that Chloe was sensibly dressed and had a good sun hat. They both took binoculars and Chloe carried a camera with a long lens. They walked for about an hour and a half in a circle which included some of the 'Tana River'. Chloe was very enthusiastic and recorded all the birds that she observed and the few game animals. Chloe was frightened of the hippos and crocodiles in the river. She was terrified of a three foot monitor lizard which shot across their path. She clutched Polly to her. Polly was slightly embarrassed, but did not say anything. However when they got back for a late breakfast, Chloe seemed to have totally recovered. After breakfast Chloe seemed happy to write up her journal which allowed Polly time to do various administrative jobs around the camp.

They had a light lunch and Chloe asked if she could sunbathe. She was worried that it might upset some of the staff. Polly explained that none of them were Moslems, and so she did not think any of them cared. Chloe asked Polly to join her, but Polly declined saying she had a lot of book work to do. She did not let on that she was doing a large amount of the financial recording to save money with the accountants.

The hunting party arrived home in the late afternoon. Ret was pleased, as he had shot a bull buffalo. Gideon whispered to Polly that it was not a very good trophy, but it was good enough. They both were relieved that Ret was a good shot. He had said that he had experience with shooting bison in the USA. Polly thought they had to take him on trust, as it would have been rather rude to insist that he did some shooting practice, after he had sighted in his rifle.

Dinner that night was excellent. Josiah made very good use of the buffalo's liver which was not over cooked and tasted wonderful. All the staff were pleased with the excess of fresh meat for roasting. There was also a large amount of biltong prepared.

The next day Ret and Gideon set off after an elephant. Chloe elected to come, as it was very unlikely that they would find a big enough tusker on the first day and so there would actually be no killing. She sat next to Polly who sat in the middle of the three seats in the middle of the Landrover. Hak sat on her other side. It was quite a squash. Polly was slightly embarrassed as Chloe rested her hand on Polly's bare thigh and occasionally would stroke her. It gave Polly the creeps, but she didn't know what to do. She could not get away from Chloe without invading Hak's space or making a fuss. Luckily they found some fresh elephant spoor so Ret, Gideon and Hak got out of the Landrover to follow the elephants on foot. They took food and water. Polly, Chloe and Noah soon found a good spot by the river to have lunch. It was on a high bank and there were several big trees. They could see Hippos in the water. Polly reassured Chloe that there was no danger. Polly explained that Hippos were particularly dangerous, when they had come on to the land to forage at night, and then, if you got between them and the water, they would charge.

Chloe did relax and they had an extended lunch bird watching. They were also lucky, as four giraffe came down to drink. Polly was so relieved there was much more room in the Landrover on the way home. She was also pleased, as the following day she took Chloe on another walking safari. Once again Chloe tried to encourage Polly to sunbathe with her in the afternoon. It was difficult for Polly to find an excuse, so she did join her and was very embarrassed as Chloe wanted her to put sun cream on her back. Polly was so pleased that she had a good tan and did not need any cream. Polly did not like it that Chloe always seemed to be watching her. In fact it annoyed her so much that Polly went to her tent, saying that she was too hot. Polly would not have found it nearly as embarrassing if it had been Ret ogling her. She would just have thought he was a dirty old man. Chloe looking at her, unnerved her.

Things came to a head one night. Polly was asleep and something woke her. She immediately realised that she was not alone in the tent. She was about to shout for the night watchman, thinking it was a thief, when Chloe said softly,

"Can I come in bed with you? I'm so frightened of the Hippos."

Polly was horrified. Her initial reaction was anger, but she controlled herself and said,

"Certainly you cannot, Chloe. I will escort you back to your tent and then check up on the two night watchmen." Polly was relieved that Chloe had not turned her torch on and the generator had long since been turned off. Polly was naked and was reluctant to get out of bed with Chloe still in her tent, but she quickly got out of bed and wrapped a kikoi around her above her breasts. She turned on her torch and found her flip-flops. Then she said very sternly.

"Chloe, I am not that sort of girl. Follow me to your tent." Polly was pleased to see Baku, one of the night-watchmen, patrolling near Chloe's tent. She spoke to him softly in his language. She heard him chuckle. She turned to Chloe and said,

"Baku says there is not a hippo for ten miles, but he will watch. You have nothing to fear." Chloe did not reply, but just went into her tent and zipped up the flap.

Polly returned to her bed. Her mind was in turmoil. *'Did she look like a lesbian? Perhaps Chloe was really frightened of the hippos. If so, why had she not gone to her father's tent? Had she done the right thing? Had she lost them a client? She hated the idea of telling Roly the reason, why they had lost the clients.'* Eventually she went back to sleep. She was dead to the world in the morning and did not hear the hunting party leaving.

Josiah woke her with some tea as normal. She quickly dressed and did her normal duties before going to the mess tent for breakfast. Chloe was already there. She had obviously been crying. In normal

25

circumstances if a girl friend was crying, Polly would have put her arm around her to comfort her. She was repelled by going anywhere near Chloe. Mercifully Josiah took quite a time to sort out breakfast. When they were alone, Polly said,

"Chloe, why are you crying?"

"I thought you loved me. Please don't tell my father about last night."

"I won't say a word. Does your father know about your inclinations?"

"No, he doesn't, but I think he has guessed. I think he would be very angry." Polly sighed,

"Well I suggest we carry on as normal. Rest assured Baku will not say anything. However I suggest you keep your distance from me and that we do not sit next to one another in the Landrover. Would you like to go on a game walk after breakfast?"

Chloe sniffed and replied,

"Thank you Polly you are so kind. Yes I would like a walk."

So life went on. However Polly found sleeping rather difficult. She was nervous that Chloe would come again on some other pretext. She wished she had someone to discuss it with. Her thoughts went to Dick. She longed to give him a hug. She longed for him to stroke her hair, as she knew then that somehow her problems would seem to disappear.

Eventually the Safari reached a successful conclusion. Ret was delighted. He gave Gideon a large tip which pleased Polly. It was only after they had left that Polly found a simple note from Chloe. It read,

'Polly you are so beautiful. Please buy yourself something pretty with this. All my love Chloe.'

Polly tore up the note into tiny pieces. She was appalled by the large amount of money, but she put it into the safe, thinking, *'every bit helps.'*

Chapter 4

New clients

She had to go out to a dinner party with Roly. He kissed her, as she was getting out of her Landrover. She could not really avoid it, but she thought at least he is a guy. Auntie Margaret called for lunch one day. Polly would have liked to have talked to her about Chloe's behaviour, but she thought that Auntie Margaret would just be totally shocked and then very unhelpful.

Polly was pleased that at least the next Safari was for two men from Sweden who each wanted to shoot a lion. This was potentially very lucrative, as they could hunt from the ranch and she could charge the local ranchers for killing any stock-taking lions.

The Swedes called Sven and Henkie were in their sixties and were very overweight. They seemed delighted to be met by Polly. There was a lot of what Polly thought of as, harmless banter with some sexual innuendos. She was just so pleased they were men, and so was happy to go along with the laughs. She had stopped wearing shorts and low tops, when the problem with Chloe occurred, but now she was pleased to wear them. Wearing trousers and shirts had been very hot.

As they had never shot anything other than rabbits before, Polly and Gideon really put them through their paces with the guns. Mercifully they were very sensible and not arrogant. Polly was pleased that they obviously respected Gideon. However Polly and Gideon were very well aware that even the bravest of men could turn to jelly, when they are charged by a lion. The main thing was to make sure that they shot the lion fatally with the first shot.

After three days, word came in that a big lion had killed a steer on a nearby ranch. They all got in the Landrover to have a look at the kill. Gideon wisely brought three of the staff to prepare the site. He wanted to make sure the hunters would have a good field of fire. Thorn brush was cut so that the lion would be encouraged to continue his feast of the dead steer with his flank to the hunter.

Gideon briefed Sven and Henkie, where they were going to sit. They had tossed a coin to decide who was going to be first. Henkie had won. Sven would be armed, but only for self protection. Gideon would take the third shot, if Henkie made an error with the first two shots. Polly would be in charge of the big torch light on its tripod.

They had an early high tea so that they were on site well before dusk. They had to prepare for a long boring wait, so that camp chairs, thermos flasks of coffee, bottles of water and sandwiches had been brought. Once they were all settled, there was to be no more talking. They were lucky. The lion came soon after 10.00 pm. They did not hear him come, but they heard the crunching of bones. Polly waited for Henkie's touch on her arm, as he slowly got to his feet. She turned on the lamp. Henkie killed the lion with a single shot into the heart, just behind the shoulder. He had one death throw and then he was still. No one moved. There were two courses of action. Henkie could fire again to ascertain that the lion was definitely dead, or they could wait. They waited and then Gideon walked up to corpse with his gun at the ready. The lion was definitely dead. Henkie was delighted. They all returned to base and the skinners were dispatched. The sooner the skin was cured the better.

The whole camp relaxed in a holiday type mood, waiting for another lion kill to be reported. Four days later another local rancher rang. Sadly, when they visited the kill, Gideon could see that it was only a lioness and not the trophy that they had hoped for. Gideon and Polly went out and killed it to earn some money. Polly did not bother to tell Lady Standup!

It was another five days before Sven could claim his trophy. Although he was pleased, Polly was rather sad. She knew it was part of the job, but all this killing was getting to her. She longed to start her dream of taking photographic safaris.

Polly decided to have a small dinner party on the Swedes last night, as a bit of a celebration. She invited Roly, as she thought it would be a good PR exercise. Sadly Dick could not come, as he was away in the NFD blood testing cattle. She invited Ophelia who was hesitant at first, but when she heard Dick would not be coming, she agreed to come. Polly arranged for Roly to give Ophelia a lift. Polly was highly amused that Sven and Henkie made a big fuss of Ophelia. The dinner party was a great success.

Their next client was another American. He wanted to shoot a large number of species of plains game. Polly had taken a hunting block in Masailand just north of the Tanzanian border to the East of the Masai Mara. There was very little tracking or real hunting involved and so Polly found this slaughter even more sickening. The fifty year old client called Donald was a kind man and so Polly found it strange that he wanted to shoot so many beautiful antelope. Apparently he owned a hunting lodge in the Rockies and wanted all these trophies to go on the walls.

One morning after the hunting party had left; Polly was walking behind the mess tent, as she had seen a hole low down in the canvas during dinner on the previous night. She slipped on the loose shingle. As she fell, her right thigh caught the metal tent peg and her fall drove it up the leg of her shorts into her groin. It really hurt, but she didn't cry out. Then, as she got to her feet there seemed to be blood everywhere. It poured down her leg. She hobbled round the tent and almost fell into Josiah, as she felt so weak. Josiah saw the blood and gave a shout and their seemed to be staff all around her. Josiah held a white napkin tight in her groin which seemed to stem the blood. They carried her to her bed and laid a towel under her. Polly had known Josiah as an old man all her life. She had no worries as he took her shorts off to see the extent of the cut. Polly could see immediately that it needed stitching. She did not feel so weak now that she was lying down.

Polly was in a dilemma. She did not think that her wound was serious enough to warrant calling the flying doctor. However she did not relish the drive to Nairobi which would take a full day. She knew there was likely to be some sort of hospital at Narok, but that was two and a half hours away and she thought the facilities would be rather poor. Luckily Gideon had driven the client, so Noah was available. She had heard that there was a veterinary research station at Aitong which was only an hour away. She wondered if they would stitch her up. She thought the best idea was for her to get on the radio. She knew the veterinary department had a special time when they organised the various vaccination teams.

She was still holding the napkin tightly into groin. The bleeding seemed to have stopped, but she felt a little light headed, when she got up. She hobbled to the radio in Gideon's tent. She was grateful for his efficiency. It was all set up. All she had to do was to turn it on. Even the various networks were labelled on the frequency dial. She switched on and moved the dial to the veterinary frequency. She felt faint and slumped in a chair. As she listened, to her delight and relief, she heard Dick's voice. She was cross with herself as she started to cry. She did not know the correct radio procedure, so she pushed the send switch and said,

"This is Polly the hunter to Dick the vet, over."

The radio was amazingly clear and Dick could hear a catch in her voice. He replied,

"Polly from Dick, how can I help you?" Polly was so cross with herself as she knew she sounded like an eight year old,

"Dick I'm camped with a client near the Tanzanian border. I fell this morning and cut my leg. It is rather a big gnash and I think it needs stitching, but I don't want to bother the flying doctor."

"I'm in the area on Rinderpest campaign. I'm happy to stitch you up. You have then no need to drive to Nairobi."

"Oh Dick, if you could that would be marvellous. The camp is a little hard to find so I will get Noah to wait on the main road to guide you in."

"Hopefully I will be with you in an hour. I should lie down and relax. Dick, over and out."

Polly hobbled back to her bed and lay down. She felt so much better. Josiah brought her a cup of tea and she told him what was happening. Dick was always popular with the African staff. Josiah laughed and said he would make a good lunch for him.

Polly was now totally relaxed and dozed off to sleep. She woke, when she heard the vehicles arriving. It was only then that she realised that she did not have any shorts on. She felt suddenly weak and thought, '*it is too late now. At least my knickers are not too skimpy!*'

She sat up and felt a little faint. Dick came into her tent.

"You are a poor girl! I should lie down as you look a little pale."

"Oh Dick, I'm so pleased to see you. Can you give me a hug?"

She felt so much better, when she felt his strong arms around her. As they broke apart, they made eye contact. Dick gave her a gentle kiss on the lips. Polly gave him a cheeky smile.

"It's lucky you are not a medical doctor, as I think you can be struck off for being too familiar with your patients!" Dick answered,

"Now let's have a look at the wound. Are you up to date with tetanus vaccination?"

"Yes, I was given a booster in the UK."

Dick gently peeled away the napkin. He could see it certainly needed stitching. It was a deep six inch cut which went up into her groin. He could not see the top of it as it was hidden by her knickers. The haemorrhage had stopped. Dick said,

"The bleeding has stopped, but you are right it certainly needs stitching. I'm afraid the first injection of the local will sting a little, but then I will inject through the frozen area and so hopefully you won't feel anything. I have to be gentle with horses or they tend to kick me in the teeth, so hopefully I will be gentle with you. I will get a bowl of water from Josiah and another towel so that I can clean the wound first. There is bound to be some contamination, so I will leave a small hole at the bottom of the wound so that any infection can drain out. I have also got some antibiotic tablets for you to take."

Polly lay back, as he went out of the tent. He came back with a clean towel and a bowl. He then disappeared again to get his kit. He had an old fashioned doctor's bag. He got out some cotton wool and some antiseptic. He smiled at Polly.

"I think you have lost a little blood and so you are suffering a bit of shock, which is why you felt a little weak. I should just lie back."

Polly found he was very gentle. In fact it was not at all unpleasant. She was slightly alarmed when he said,

"Sorry Polly, I'm going to have to take your knickers off. The cut has gone right up into your groin." To hide her nerves she replied,

"I imagine you have had a lot of experience, taking girl's knickers off." She was not sure that she was reassured by his reply of,

"I wish!" As she raised her bottom and felt him gently pull off her pants. She smiled to herself, when she remembered the old musical joke of wearing clean knickers in case you got run over by a bus! Then he said,

"You will feel a little prick, and then it will sting before it goes numb."

She clenched her fist, as she felt the needle. There was a stinging sensation and then she felt nothing except the odd amount of pressure as Dick injected all along the two edges of the cut. She was looking down at the top of his head, as he got higher up her leg. She felt his hand, as he gently pushed her thighs a little wider. She wondered why she didn't feel embarrassed. He looked up and they made eye contact. He gave her a lovely smile.

"That's got enough local in. Hopefully you won't feel anything more except in a couple of hours, when the local wears off. Then you will feel some tingling. Have you ever had an injection at the dentist?"

"No I was lucky. I was born with good teeth."

Then Polly could only see the top of his head as he was stitching her leg. He kept chatting,

"I'm afraid you are going to have a scar, when you wear a bikini, but no one will see anything in shorts." As he finished he looked up at her saying,

"Although I shouldn't say it, I have made a very neat job of that."

He bobbed down and Polly felt a little kiss on a very private part of her which wasn't anaesthetised. In horror she said,

"Dick that was really naughty!" Looking up again he sighed

"Sorry I just couldn't resist it. You have been an amazingly brave young lady."

Polly grabbed both his ears. She could not stop smiling at him.

"I will remember that very naughty kiss to my dying day. You are a complete rogue. I suppose that you are not all bad. At least you did not take my clothes off, when I was eight after the calving. You just waited until I was eighteen to do much worse!"

Nothing more was said. Polly got up, when he went out of the tent, and she put on a clean pair of knickers and shorts. She felt slightly light headed, but otherwise OK. Lunch was good fun. She loved hearing all his funny stories. When he went to leave he stressed to her that she should put the least stress on the suture line as possible, until the stitches came out. He gave her some antibiotics to take. He hung his head as he finally came to leave.

"I don't think I deserve a hug?" She held out her arms and replied,

"You have done a great stitching job. You are forgiven, but I will be expecting more appropriate and professional behaviour when the stitches come out."

They hugged and Dick was relieved to feel her pull him tight to her. He thought, '*What a wonderful girl. Does it matter that I am fifteen years older than her. She came with Roly to the Muthaiga Ball. I'm sure he is older than me.*'

It was two weeks later, when Polly rang him to say that she had just got home and the client had left. Would he like some lunch the next day. Dick said he would love some.

Polly laughed to herself on the next morning, as she put on her prettiest knickers. '*I'm a complete tart. Why do I fancy him so much? He is old enough to be my father. I suppose it was love at first sight. I loved him, when I first met him, when I was only eight!*'

Polly remembered to tell Josiah that Dick was coming to lunch. She warned him with a laugh that Dick was nearly always late.

Sure enough it was well after tea time, when he arrived. Dick expected Polly to be cross, but instead she gave him a big hug and said,

"Can you stay for supper? If you get a call perhaps I can come with you."

"Oh Polly, that is so kind of you."

She sat with him, when he ate his lunch. He ate as if he hadn't had food for a month. He did admit to her that he didn't get time to have breakfast, as he got an early call. She longed to look after him. '*What was the matter with her? She was getting all maternal now.*'

After he had eaten he asked, if he could have a shower. Polly had given most of her of her father's clothes to the staff, but she managed to find a pair of shorts and a shirt for Dick. She had a tear in her eye, when he came on to the veranda. He guessed what the problem was. He sat in an easy chair and said,

"Come and sit on my lap and I can give you a hug. You must still miss your Dad?"

As he stroked her hair she quietly sobbed,

"Yes, I do. I hoped it would get better, but it doesn't" Dick replied,

"Look at me, I still miss my Dad. He died nearly ten years ago."

Polly looked at him and could see his tears. It made her feel in some way better. She dried her eyes and said,

"Come on. You had better take my stitches out while you are feeling a bit down. I don't trust you to take my knickers off, when you are feeling all hale and hearty."

She got up off his knee and led him through to her bedroom. She lay on the bed feeling very wanton, while he went out to his car to get a pair of scissors and some forceps. When he came back again he said,

"I don't think I was totally to blame for that naughty kiss. You do look incredibly sexy lying on your back with your legs apart."

"I'm not taking any of the blame. You took my knickers off and pushed my legs wider apart and I was in a weakened state from blood loss! Come on let's get on with it?"

Dick thought she looked even sexier as she wriggled out of her shorts and then her knickers. Her legs were wide apart, but she covered herself with one hand. Polly had forgotten that she was quite ticklish. She started to giggle, as he took the stitches out. He had just one more to remove from high up in her groin.

"You will just have to move your hand for me to remove the last stitch."

"It is your entire fault. I was not shy until you gave me that kiss."

She removed her hand and opened her legs as far as she could.

"Come on. You have seen it all before!"

Dick's hands were shaking, when he eventually got the last stitch. She jumped off the bed and very sexily got back into her knickers and shorts. Dick did not look away. She pushed him out of the bedroom saying,

"You are real trouble Dick. I don't know what I'm going to do with you. I just so love teasing you. I have never cut myself before. I will have to make sure I never do again. I did look with a mirror yesterday. You certainly did a good job. I don't think I will have a scar. Certainly whoever is looking should not be that close. Now I have a serious question to ask you."

She told him all about Chloe and asked him what else she should have done, to have averted her coming to her tent. Dick was not sure what she should have done. He said it was way outside his experience. He then told her a funny story about the Swedish Minister for Foreign Aid. Dick had been told by his boss to fly this guy who was gay, around the various livestock projects that they were helping to finance. They had stayed on a ranch, where they had separate bedrooms in a rondavel, but had to share a bathroom. Dick said he had been very nervous, when he went to bed. He was even more nervous, when there were screams from the bathroom. He went to investigate, only to find the man standing on a chair. There was a scorpion in the bath. Dick had grabbed a bottle off the side of the bath and was killing the scorpion, there were even more screams. Apparently he was using a very expensive bottle of aftershave!

Polly loved this story. How was it that Dick could always cheer her up? She had already asked him to stay for supper. Then she asked him if he would like to stay the night, as he had said he had a visit to do at Machakos in the morning. With a twinkle in his eye, but a very straight face he asked if he could share her bed, as he was very frightened of hippos. This earned him a very sharp rebuke,

"No you jolly well can't! I'm not sure I trust you to give me a kiss good night."

As it was they had a lovely evening and they had a lingering kiss, when they said goodnight.

Dick went to sleep immediately, but Polly could not settle. She so longed to creep into his room and cuddle up with him. She wished she was frightened of hippos! Eventually she slept.

They were both sad in the morning. They were both busy people and had demanding jobs. They could not find a time when they could meet again.

Chapter 5

A trip to Kitali

It was six weeks later, when Polly heard Dick on the phone on Thursday night.

"Do you fancy a game of hockey? It is the first game of the rugby season. I'm playing for 'Nondescripts' away in Kitali on Saturday. The girls are taking a hockey team up there. So we can make a weekend of it, I have got a job to do on the way. I have got to go and take a look at a sick Roschild Giraffe at Soy tomorrow. They will put us up at Soy Country Club. Sorry it is at such short notice."

"I would love to come, but I am rubbish at hockey. I played lacrosse at school."

"We won't tell anyone that. With those lovely legs of yours, I bet you can run like a stag."

"I certainly can run. I'm not sure about lovely legs, but I can assure you that you are the only man who has ever seen all of them!"

"Can you get to my house at Kabete for breakfast? It is at Lower Kabete. It is the house directly opposite the Central Artificial Insemination Station (CAIS) which is well signed posted. I have got to collect some semen before breakfast at 7.00 am, so I should be home by 8.00 am."

"Can I come and help you. I'm good in the mornings I can easily get to you before 7.00 am."

"I'd love that. See you at 7.00." He rang off.

Polly was really delighted and excited. First she had to find her lacrosse clothes and her shoes. She had never bothered even to open the big packing case which had eventually arrived from her Aunt in Norwich. She really laughed, when she saw the dark green thick pants that she had to wear under her short, little, green, sports dress. Dick would have a real mission to get into those pants, particularly, when she found the white knickers which she used to wear underneath them. She was not too fazed about playing hockey, as she had played in Kenya until she was sixteen. She had only stopped

36

playing, when she went to the UK. She wondered what the other girls would be like. She had been so concentrated on running her father's safari business that she had not bothered to contact her old school friends. She was very much the youngest at the Muthaiga Ball. She guessed her school friends would have thought it was very fuddy duddy. She had been obliged to go to keep Roly and her Aunt happy. She wondered what she should wear for Saturday night. She guessed long, as the girls were making a weekend of it. However she threw in a very short black dress which she knew she looked good in.

She guessed Dick would want to look to see if her scar showed. Actually she was rather proud of her scar. It was very faint and barely visible, as a line pointing up to her groin. It was only when it was above the line of where her leg came from her bikini that the scar really showed. It looked like an arrow pointing at her bush. She suddenly blushed, thinking about Dick following the arrow to where he had kissed her. He was a very naughty boy, but she knew she looked at him through rose-tinted spectacles, and that he could do no wrong. She would have to behave herself. It would have been easier, if she hadn't loved him so much. She was such a baby. She only cried, when he was around.

She sailed through Nairobi early in the morning, as it was long before the traffic had built up. She was ten minutes early at his house. She walked boldly in, as the side door was open. She heard Dick laughing in Swahili with his cook, saying he was taking the prettiest girl in the world away for the weekend. His cook asked him how he was going to afford the bride price. Polly guessed he was a Kikuyu and answered in Kikuyu,

"Sadly my father has died, but he told me that I was to save myself for man who had so many cattle that no man could count them. Do you think this animal doctor will ever get that many cattle?" The old cook laughed and replied in Kikuyu,

"One thing is certain you are the prettiest girl in the world. I am called Mobia. I will feed him well. It is then up to him how he manages to get the cattle. Would you like a cup of tea? The master is still drinking his and the kettle is hot?" Polly answered in Kikuyu,

"I am called Polly and I would love a cup of tea."

As Mobia turned to go to the kitchen to bring her a cup of tea, Dick said,

"I had forgotten that you spoke some of the tribal languages. You have a great gift. What did Mobia say?"

"Basically he doesn't rate your chances of raising my bride price!" Dick laughed,

"I will keep dreaming."

They drank their tea and walked over to the CAIS. They put on the waterproofs provided and walked behind two Sahiwal bulls that were being led to the collection building. They were led on halters by just one man. It seemed as if they knew the form.

In the collection building the bull's halters were secured. Polly went with Dick, as he prepared the microscope and what he called a 'heated stage'. He said it was important that the little tiny spermatozoa did not get cold. There were two large leather and rubber tubes, bigger than a man's arm hanging on the wall. Polly asked what they were. Dick told her they were artificial vaginas. Polly whispered,

"Wow!" Dick explained that they needed them, when they were collecting semen from European bulls which were often called 'Grade' bulls. That was an easy task. They would mount a wooden 'make believe' cow and serve into an artificial vagina. The artificial vagina had warm water in a sleeve so it felt to the bull like a real vagina. Dick whispered to her,

"Take that naughty smirk off your face. You will upset the bulls. They take themselves very seriously."

Then he told her that Indian or African bulls with humps, like Sahiwals and Borans were different. They would not serve a dummy cow. Therefore they had to collect their semen by electro-ejaculation. Polly looked perplexed. Dick explained that was what they were going to do now.

A large, metal, torpedo shaped, rod was pushed into the bull's rectum. Polly was surprised that the bull did not seem to mind and continued to eat some maize stalks which had been put in front of it. Dick introduced Joseph who was the chief collector. Polly realised that he was a Wakamba. She greeted him in his own language. He beamed with pleasure. Joseph took his position just behind the front leg of the bull looking towards the bull's tail. He held a beaker under the prepuce of the bull. Dick took the control box of the electro-ejaculator and was holding the instrument in the bull's rectum.

He pressed a switch and counted, one, two, three. Then he released the switch and counted, one, two, three. Then he pressed the switch again, counting again. He did that sequence three times.

Polly watched the bull closely. When he pressed the switch, the bull hunched his strong back and gave a loud grunt before sighing, when Dick released the switch. The third time the bull's penis shot out and he ejaculated into the beaker. Joseph took the ejaculate to the warm water bath at blood heat. Dick took the ejaculator out of the bull's rectum. The bull continued to eat the maize. She was sure he had a rather smug smile on his face.

After Dick and Joseph had examined the semen and were satisfied with its quality. Joseph was tasked to dilute it and to make as many straws for insemination into cows, as possible.

Dick washed and disinfected the ejaculator and then they repeated the same procedure with the second bull. Polly was impressed by the power of the two bulls. She was amazed that with just one thrust they ejaculated. She had watched two lions mate, when her father was alive. They had seemed to copulate for hours. She rightly supposed that bulls were typical of herbivores. They had to mate quickly or a lion would catch them. Lions could take all the time they liked.

They set off after a quick breakfast. They had over two hundred miles to do, but the tarmac was good. They travelled on the main road North East to Uganda. It was only when they got to Soy that they had to turn right on to the Kitali Road.

They had stopped at a café in Nakuru for some lunch. Polly enjoyed the journey. Dick was a fountain of information. She had always been interested in animals. She asked him if she was right, in thinking that bulls had to be quick, when mating, because they were frightened of being caught by a lion. Dick explained that also a bull would have several cows in his harem, so he had a lot of work to do. Polly teased him saying.

"I bet you wish you had been born a bull." Dick smiled,

"No. I will be happy with just one heifer." It was Polly's turn to smile.

"I think you can learn a lot from those bulls. I think most heifers don't just want one thrust." She demonstrated by grasping her left bicep and punching her left forearm forward and then continued,

39

"One of those bulls definitely had a very smug look on his face after he had ejaculated. I don't think any heifer would like that." Dick replied,

"If a bull found a certain heifer totally irresistible and kissed her on a very intimate place. How should he make amends?" Polly really laughed then.

"I think young heifers are rather easily surprised. I think when they don't feel so vulnerable they might have enjoyed the kiss. I think the bull should be very patient with the heifer and show that he is really fond of her not just wanting to...." Polly demonstrated a thrust with her forearm again.

Dick continued to drive with a very pensive look on his face.

They arrived at Soy Country Club. There were three men sitting at a table. They were obviously the guys that Dick had come to help. Dick introduced himself and introduced Polly, as a friend who was very knowledgeable about game animals. The oldest man called Gilfred asked Polly, if she was Hector Cavendish's daughter. She replied that she was. She surprised herself, as she had no desire to cry, even when, Gilfred said what a great man her father was.

Gilfred then said,

"We are really grateful to you Dick. Let's go and look at your patient. She is only a ten minute drive away. She had a calf two days ago and she has not managed to get up since. We have seen the calf suck from her several times. She rolls on her side to let him get to her teats. Now sadly she can't even sit up on to her brisket. We have had a guard on her at a distance just in case there are any predators."

They drove off in the two Landrovers with Dick following. Dick said to Polly,

"I don't hold a lot of hope for the poor giraffe. It sounds as if she has a fracture of a femur or her pelvis."

"That's sad. Let's hope you don't have to shoot her. Her poor calf needs his Mum."

Dick reached across and squeezed her hand. She gave him a beautiful smile, saying,

"Thanks."

They left the vehicles on the road and set off into the bush. They were met by the guard. Polly guessed he was either a Nandi or a Kipsigis. They had very similar languages. Polly greeted him. He rushed to shake her hand. Dick was not surprised, but the other men were, particularly, as Polly continued to chat to him in his language, as the two of them walked, hand in hand towards the giraffe. Polly was carrying some of Dick's equipment. Dick was carrying the rest. The guard took the equipment from her. Polly teased him saying carrying heavy loads was a woman's job. He laughed replying that was the African way, but it was not the European way!

The giraffe was lying flat out. She was breathing very slowly. Polly could see by the look on Dick's face that he thought that things were pretty hopeless. He listened to her heart and then handed the stethoscope to Polly, so that she could have a listen.

"I have not listened to a giraffe's heart before, but I think that is seriously slow."

He then took the giraffe's rectal temperature which he said was subnormal. He took the stethoscope back from Polly and listened to the left flank of the giraffe which was upper most. He said to Polly,

"There is very little rumen movement. I'm sure that I am missing something. I will have a feel in her rectum to see if there are any fractures in there, before we palate her legs."

He lubricated his arm with some jell. As he was feeling inside the animal, Polly lent forward and whispered,

"Can I have a feel?"

"Of course you can. Lubricate your arm really well, as she is terribly dry in there. She must be very dehydrated. There is at least some good news. I cannot feel any fractures in her pelvis."

Polly put her arm inside the giraffe. All she could feel was dry dung. So she had to take Dick's word for it that there were no fractures.

Then Dick worried her, as he started to manipulate the giraffe's enormously powerful legs. She was worried that he was going to get kicked. She remembered her father telling her that a giraffe could kill a lion with a kick with its hind leg. Suddenly Dick's face lit up,

"Polly I'm such a fool. I know what her problem is. She has got milk fever which is a temporary crisis in her blood calcium levels."

He got out a large bottle, of what he said was a calcium solution. He attached a long tube to the bottle and asked the guard to stand behind the giraffe's neck, and hold it for him. Then he asked Polly to kneel on the giraffe's neck. He then pushed an enormous needle into

41

the giraffe's jugular vein. Blood poured out. Polly though, *'It's lucky that I don't faint at the sight of blood or I would be flat out now!'*

He attached the tube from the bottle to the needle. He told the guard to turn the bottle upside down. Polly could see that the liquid was running, as there were bubbles coming into the bottle. The bottle was nearly empty, when Polly felt the giraffe stiffen. She shouted,

"Look out, Dick."

With that the giraffe swung its massive neck off the ground and lifted Polly about six feet into the air, as if she was a small child. She landed on her bottom. The giraffe got to its feet and galloped off. Its calf soon joined her. Dick called to Polly,

"Are you OK?" He ran to her, but she was up on her feet, before he reached her. She was smiling,

"I'm fine. I landed on my bottom. I will have a big bruise tomorrow. You will certainly not be seeing that." Dick whispered in her ear,

"You have such a lovely petite little bottom." Polly giggled,

"A compliment like that might get you a very private viewing of my bruise after all."

Gilfred and his colleagues were really grateful. The guard thought Dick was a miracle worker. Polly and Dick drove back to Soy Country Club. Polly congratulated him. Dick said how sorry he was that he had put her at risk. He said he was cross with himself, as he should not have been so cavalier.

Polly squeezed his arm,

"Anyhow there was no harm done and the whole escapade has given me an idea for my future. I'm getting upset with the hunting. I hate all this killing. I had thought that I wanted to take up photographic safaris, but I don't think that I have got the patience. Also I don't really find it exciting enough. I have just had an idea. Do you think I could set up a game catching business? Also I thought, before your marvellous bit of veterinary work that there was going to be an orphan giraffe to look after. I would love to look after orphans. What do you think?" Dick replied instantly,

"I think it is a great idea. I would enjoy helping you with the darting. I think we would make a great team." Polly laughed,

"You are not saying that because you feel guilty about my bruised bottom? Really it is nothing."

"I promise it has nothing to do with that. I would really love working with you."

Polly's heart missed a beat, as she knew that he meant it.

When they got back to Soy Country Club, they checked in. They were shown to one of the beautiful en suite chalets. After the receptionist had left, Polly said,

"You old rogue, Dick. We have got a double bed."

"I promise that I didn't plan it." Rather pensively Polly replied,

"I think I believe you. At least it is a big bed. We will have to have strict ground rules. I'm going to have this side furthest from the door and you are not allowed in my half."

"Even if I get frightened of the wild animals in the night?" She punched him playfully.

"You stay on that side, come hell or high water! Now I'm going to have a bath and change. I do not need my back scrubbing."

Dick was lying on his side of the bed reading a book, when she came out of the bathroom wrapped in a towel, looking delightfully pink. Her long blond hair was also wrapped in a towel.

"OK, it's your turn. Shall I wear a dress tonight?"

"I'd love that."

When he came out, she was sitting on his side of the bed brushing her hair. She looked lovely in her short black dress. Dick pointed to the bed.

"That's my side!" She gave him a dazzling smile.

"Sorry the hair drier wouldn't reach to my side. You men are so lucky having short hair. Shall I cut mine off?"

"Please don't. You have such beautiful long hair. That dress really suits you. You look great." Polly chuckled,

"What you really mean is that it is so short you can almost see my knickers. Actually I'm quite miffed that you have not asked to see my scar." Dick smiled,

"I'm on my best behaviour. I was told on the way up here that I must not surprise or frighten you. I do listen, you know."

Polly jumped up and said,

"You have been a real gent. Come on let's go and eat. I'm starving."

As they went out the door, Dick's hand brushed her bottom,

"Is it sore?"

"No it isn't actually, but it is still out of bounds."

They had a really lovely meal. Dick did not have anything other than water, as he said that any drink before a game definitely took the edge off his performance. Polly said she would only have water to keep him company. She said she was going to play very badly anyway. Everyone would think she had been drinking. It was quite early, as they walked to their chalet. It was chilly. Polly lent towards him and he put his arm around her shoulders. She felt rather little, but also very loved. It was a nice feeling. They were both shy when they got ready for bed. They each were wrapped in kikois and they each stuck to their correct side of the bed. Dick said,

"OK if I turn the light out?"

"Yes fine, sleep well."

"I hope you do as well."

They were both pretty tired after the drive and they soon were asleep. Dick was the first to wake in the morning. To his horror, he found Polly lying on top of him. He thought he would be reprimanded, because he had moved on to her side of the bed. Then he relaxed, as he realised he was on his side of the bed. His kikoi was still around his waist, but Polly had managed to lose hers and so was naked in his arms. He stroked her hair. She kissed his neck and said,

"My excuse is that I was a little cold, but if I'm truthful, I really wanted a hug. I could grow to like sleeping with you. You are so warm and cuddly." She kissed his neck again.

"I love kissing that little place." Dick said,

"Can I put my hands there?" His hands gently rested on her bottom. "There is nowhere else to put them." She murmured,

"That is a lie, but you can. It is not sore. We will have a look later to see if I have got a bruise. I would be mortified, if the other girls thought that you beat me! That would be really unfair on you. I think you are a little embarrassed that you are so much older than me. You mustn't be. I just don't find younger guys attractive. I expect it is because my father was so important in my life."

She felt him kiss the top of her head. She wriggled up him and they kissed on the lips. Their lips parted and their tongues played together. It was suddenly too much for Dick. He rolled her on to her back and kissed her passionately. She could not stop herself from responding. She had her arms tightly around his neck. Eventually they broke apart. He expected her to be cross or at least shy, but he did not expect her to say,

"That was bloody lovely. I had the hots for you when I was eight. I still have them ten years later. I was going to give you a ticking off, saying that you had pulled my kikoi off, but I did it myself. I so wanted to feel your body next to mine. I am sorry I am such a wanton hussy. Will you forgive me?"

Dick did not answer, but kissed her again. Then he rolled on to his back and she came back in his arms as before. Then they lay in companionable silence, each knowing a bridge had been crossed. It was no longer, if they were going to be lovers, but rather, when they were going to be lovers. Soon they decided to get up. Polly said,

"I'm shy of you seeing me in the nude." Then she smiled.

"My excuse for letting you see me naked, is so you can check on my bruise. She got out of bed and stood before him. Slowly she turned around saying,

"What do you think?"

"There is not a blemish on you. You do not bruise as easily as you thought. Turn around and let me see your scar."

"Now I am shy." However she gave herself away by giving a little giggle.

"No you are not shy. In fact I think you are rather proud of it."

She turned to face him and moved nearer to the bed. He lent forward.

"It is like an arrow telling me where to kiss you. I think it is pretty. Yesterday you gave me a lecture saying you were surprised and shocked. Please will you come a little bit nearer to me?"

Polly put her hands behind his head and gently pulled him to her. The little kiss which he gave her sent a tiny shudder through her body. She dropped to her knees in front of him and very earnestly said,

"Are you happy with what you have seen?"

"Yes and one hundred times yes. You are so beautiful."

They both stood then smiling at each other. Neither of them wanted to break the spell, but eventually Polly said,

"Mobia said he was going to feed you so you would be strong enough to earn my bride price. I bet they do a good breakfast here." Indeed they did. It was a superb breakfast.

They packed up, but decided not to go to Kitali club, as they were so early, but continued on towards Mount Elgon which is fourteen thousand feet high and is on the border between Kenya and Uganda. On the slopes is a small village with a club with a golf course called Endebess. They stopped and ordered some lunch, but went for an hour's walk around the golf course while lunch was being prepared.

The temperature was just right. It could easily have been a summer's day in England. There was clear blue sky. Luckily they both were used to the direct sun's rays which were very powerful as they were near to the Equator.

They finished their early, light lunch and sat on the veranda of the club drinking their coffee. The golfers began to arrive. No one seemed bothered that they were not members. Then they set off on the fourteen mile drive back to Kitali. Polly asked Dick who would likely to be playing in her hockey team. He said he was not sure, but he thought about half the girls would be wives of the 'Nondescripts' rugby team in which he was playing. He thought that the rest would be younger, local Nairobi girls. Polly said she wondered if she would know any of them from school. She said she was looking forward to meeting some 'normal' girls. They both laughed.

Dick asked her what she was like as a teenage school girl. Polly said that here in Kenya she was very much like the other girls. She said she had lots of friends and was very gregarious. She admitted that, when she went to England, she had become much more serious. She said academic achievement was given a very high priority. She had found that hard. She had loved the sport. She told him he had been right, when he had been so complimentary about her legs. She actually was a good runner. She held the school record for the mile by quite a large margin. Then she laughed saying how she had changed. She said that she just could not believe that she had been happy to stand naked in front of him. She told him that Lady Standup had given her a strict talking to about spending so much time with Africans. She made Dick laugh by saying next time Lady Standup gave her a hard time, she would tell her that now she liked standing in the nude in front of European men!

46

Kitali club was really busy, when they arrived. Most of the rugby team were there. Dick rapidly introduced Polly. She received several appreciative looks from some of the team. Dick had been right about the composition of the ladies hockey team. There were five wives of rugby players. Once again Dick introduced Polly. She was immediately accepted. They all chatted away and told her about the team. Polly was introduced to two teenage girls whose dads were playing rugby who were in the team. There was a car load of four girls who had yet to arrive. Polly whispered to Dick,

"Good luck in your game. I will tag along with the girls now. I will be fine. The girls that I have met so far seem to be good fun."

Dick went to the Landrover to get his kit. When he got to the vehicle he remembered that Polly would need her stuff. He brought both bags into the club house. Polly saw him and ran to him to get her bag. She gave him a little hug which did not go unnoticed by some of the rugby team. As they went into the visitors changing room, Ken the 'Nondescript's' captain said,

"Is that your new young lady? I hope you weren't bouncing up and down on her all last night. We will have a tough game against these lads. They are always strong at home." Dick answered,

"Don't worry we had an early alcohol-free night at Soy Country Club and we both slept like logs."

"Well I'm glad to hear that. Let's hope all the team has arrived."

They all started to get changed, as Ken had a head count. He was relieved he had fifteen players. He gave them a pep talk before taking them out on to the pitch, to pass a ball around and warm up. Dick noticed the hockey girls. Polly certainly had the best legs. He saw they were still four short. However the seven girls were happily passing a couple of balls between them. He noticed they all had white shirts on, but various skirts and shorts. He looked longingly at Polly. She had on the dreaded thick green pants. She was not that far from him and obviously had felt his eyes upon her. She called out,

"These pants are bloody hot. Do you think I can take them off?"

"All of 'Nondes' would enjoy that."

With that she wriggled out of her pants, ran to the side of the pitch and threw them on the ground. Dick got tantalising glimpses of white knickers, as she ran back to join the other girls. He knew by what she had said that even the white under-pair of pants were perfectly decent, but she got a ragged cheer from the 'Nondes' players. Ken then shouted to them all,

"Forget about the girls. We've got a hard game to win."

Jim, one of the wing-forwards who was a particular friend of Dick's said,

"You've got a good girl there. She looks great fun!"

The Kitali team ran out and soon the game started. Dick had to make a real effort to stop thinking about Polly's lovely legs. As Ken had predicted, it was a hard game. 'Nondes' just managed to win by a single try. Dick was very weary, sweaty, and smelly as he staggered up the steps into the clubhouse. He nearly fell over, when Polly jumped into his arms,

"Well done. The little I saw of the game at the end was great. I saw you playing really hard. We won as well. We must have a big celebration. The four girls had to change in the car, as they were getting late. I bet you would have enjoyed travelling up with them!"

She then gave him a big kiss, before he gently let go of her thighs. A Kitali girl, who he had not met before, brought him a pint of lemonade and lime, saying,

"I went to kiss my boyfriend after a game and he pushed me away, as he said it was embarrassing." Dick replied,

"Polly is so lovely. She never embarrasses me. I'm always so proud of her." The girl held out her hand,

"I'm Kate. Do you think you are so fond of her, because you are so much older than her?"

Polly heard and butted in,

"Please don't say that Kate. He is a bit shy about our age gap."

"Well I think you are bloody lucky. He really cares for you. My boyfriend had better sharpen up or he will be on the rubbish dump!"

Dick took the lemonade and lime and staggered into the changing room. He felt his age. However a second pint of lemonade and lime, and a good shower revived him. Even so he was not prepared for Polly. She looked sensational in a long dress. It was high at the front and very low at the back. He was certain that she was, neither wearing a bra, nor knickers. In fact he had forgotten that it was the same dress which she had worn at the Muthaiga Ball. That night he had been so late and so hungry he could have been forgiven for any lapse of memory.

He longed to get her alone, but there was no chance of that, as the party was well underway and she was in the middle of a group of girls. Much to his amusement she was giving a very graphic description of the bull receiving electro-ejaculation. The girls seemed to be fascinated, particularly of Polly's demonstration of the bull thrusting and the length of his penis!

The Kitali Captain tapped his glass to get everyone's attention. He welcomed both of the 'Nondes' teams. He said how they were always pleased to have visitors, as often Kitali felt very remote from the rest of the country. He said he was sad that both of the Kitali teams had been beaten. However he said his team had beaten by foul play. The room went really quiet, as everyone thought he was going to complain about the referee. However instead, he said he thought it was totally unfair that a 'Nondes' girl had totally distracted his team by taking her knickers off and throwing them on to the ground on the side of the pitch. He said his young daughter had retrieved them. He then pulled out Polly's dark green knickers from his pocket.

"Would the young lady like to come and claim them?"

There was a massive amount of cheering. Polly showed her bravery. Although Dick could see her blushing not only on her face, but all down her back. In fact he guessed she was red all over her body. She stepped up to the captain and as he handed her the green pants, she leant forward and kissed him on the cheek. This surprised and distracted him, and so he was not prepared for her to put them on his balding head like a hat. The room went wild with cheering. In fact he continued to wear them for the rest of the evening!

She turned and looked for Dick in the crowd and immediately came to him.

"I'm so sorry, if I have embarrassed you." He gave her hug.

"It was my fault. I encouraged you to take them off." She whispered in his ear,

"You won't have to encourage me to take my knickers off tonight, as I'm not wearing any!"

"I rather hoped that was the case."

The party was a great success and went on until the early hours of the morning. Dick had previous experience of away games before. He made sure he had his and Polly's bag safely in the Landrover. He had also found out that they were staying with a couple called Jessie and Tony. They were also putting up two of the 'Nondes' hockey girls, so when it was time to go home, Dick made sure he knew which was Tony's car, as he did not have a clue where they lived. The two girls, Janine and Lucy got into Tony's car. They were just about set off when the two other girls, Louise and Peggy came running out. They had missed their lift with their hosts. They all scrambled into the front of Dick's Landrover. To make more room, much to his amusement, Polly, with some difficulty pulled up her long dress which was very figure hugging. She lifted one elegant leg over the gear stick and then repeated the procedure. When she was pressed tight up against him, he put his hand on her thigh. She said,

"This is cosy. Don't worry, Louise. I will make sure Dick's hand stays on my thigh and doesn't stray on to yours." Louise giggled.

They managed to follow Tony's car and did not get lost. When they got to the house and Jessie saw the extra girls she went into a flap.

"Oh, my goodness, I have only got two spare rooms!"

Dick thought Polly was marvellous. She said,

"Don't worry Jessie. Dick and I will sleep on the settee."

"Will you be OK? It is long enough, but it is very narrow."

"We will be fine. I will keep Dick safely under me. With all these lovely girls about, I don't want him to wander off in the night!" Louise smirked and made a thrusting gesture with her arm,

"What if he wants a bit of that? You won't be able to get away from him?" Polly laughed,

"You never know I might want a bit of that, as well. However I definitely won't let him get away with a smug look like the bull had." They all laughed.

Jessie found Polly and Dick a couple of sleeping bags. Polly smiled,

"That's great we can we can zip them together." Louise sniggered,

"I didn't think you were serious." Polly just smiled.

Dick was sitting on the settee, when they eventually were on their own. Looking at Polly he said,

"Can I take your dress off?"

"I'd love that, but can you strip first. I would like to see your reaction."

50

Dick was then shy, but eventually he was naked. Polly stood in front of him.

"There is a tiny hook and eye which you have to undo first before the zip."

She lent her neck forward to make it easier for him. She smiled as she felt his hands shaking. Then her dress slipped to the floor. She kissed him saying,

"That reaction speaks louder than words."

They kissed passionately. It was some minutes before Polly managed to get him under her in the sleeping bags. She giggled, when she told him there was no chance that he could roll her on to her tummy and give her, in Louise's words, 'a bit of that'. They definitely both would fall on the floor. They had one more kiss and then they slept.

They were still in the same position when they woke. Polly said,

"Did you have 'a bit of that'? If so you were very gentle. I didn't feel a thing!"

Dick bent his leg between her thighs and pulled her bottom to him, saying,

"You are bloody sexy."

"So are you. That feels gorgeous."

They pretended to be asleep when they heard Louise creep through to go to bathroom. When she came back, Polly could not resist saying,

"Oh Dick, you are so big!" She could only just contain her laughter long enough for Louise to get hurriedly out of the room.

Eventually they all got up and had some breakfast. Sadly Jessie had under catered, so they ran out of milk. Dick and Polly had orange juice on their cereals. There were not enough eggs, so instead of having an egg each, they had a piece of eggy bread. However although the girls were very pale and hung-over they all tried to be lively. Mercifully Polly and Dick had not had too much to drink, but just had not had enough sleep.

Polly thought it was hugely amusing, when Louise managed to be alone with her and said,

"Are you OK? Was he on top of you all night?" Polly replied,

"I'm fine. In fact I was on top of him all night and slept like a log."

Louise looked appalled and said no more.

They took the four girls back to Kitali Club in the middle of the morning. The majority of both teams were going to Endebess for lunch. Polly was delighted that Dick was very firm and they set off for the long hot journey back to Nairobi. She started to nod off to sleep before they had even reached Eldoret. Dick found some pillows so she could curl up with her head in his lap. She remembered him stroking her hair and then she slept soundly. She only woke up, when he turned off the engine at his house.

They had not had any lunch, but Dick had organised for Mobia to come in on Sunday afternoon and cook them a roast dinner. Polly ate it with relish,

"Dick this is really lovely. Thank you. I feel so bad that you drove all the way home and I did not help at all with the driving and I didn't even stay awake to help you by making conversation."

"I have so enjoyed your company. Can I persuade you to stay?" Polly smiled at him,

"I would love to stay. I'm sure no one will worry about me on the ranch, as we have not got any clients at the moment."

So they spent a very enjoyable evening. Initially Polly sat in a separate chair, but soon she got up and came and sat on his knee. They mainly talked about Polly's idea of her setting up a game trapping business.

There was no shyness, when it was time to go to bed. Polly could tell Dick was totally exhausted. They just took off their clothes and got into his bed. Polly pushed him on to his back and just lay on top of him. She gave him one kiss and he was asleep. Although she had slept in the Landrover she also was soon asleep. They both were still asleep when Mobia brought them in a cup of tea each. Because he had woken them, they had time for a shower each and a good breakfast. Dick left for work and Polly left to drive back to the ranch. She gave him a hug,

"Thank you Dick, that weekend was awesome."

To Polly's delight, Dick rang her that night at bed time.

"I just rang to say that I miss you. I couldn't think of any other excuse." Polly laughed,

"I will think up some excuse to ring you tomorrow night. Sleep well."

Chapter 6

Darting giraffe

Sadly neither of them could find a reason to meet for three weeks until Polly found an excuse.

"Dick. I have been ringing around all the possible outlets for game animals that I could think of. I have not had any luck until today. There is a zoo in Germany that is desperate to import two giraffe. At the risk of getting a big bruise on my bottom could you and I do a double act. Could you dart them and I could organise pens, transport and quarantine?"

"I would love to help you. I will see, if I can borrow a dart-gun and get the right drug. Let me know a day and I will do my very best to arrange my work around you."

"That's wonderful. Hopefully you can stay here, as I will see if I can get one of my neighbours to let us buy two giraffe off his ranch. We will still need a license for each animal from the Game Department."

"I have got a grin from ear to ear. I hope you can organise something soon. Lots of hugs." He rang off.

Polly was nervous. After their magical weekend away, she had been into a chemist in Nairobi and was amazed that she could buy contraceptive pills over the counter. She had brought three months supply. Now she was worried that Dick would think she was too forward. He had not made any attempt to make love to her. She was sure he had wanted to make love to her over that weekend; but that he was either too shy or he thought she was a girl who would not agree to sex before marriage. By taking the tablets she was saying, I'm up for it. What if he thought nice girls should not think like that. What if he thought she had had sex with lots of guys? The two things that Polly was certain about were that she wanted him and she definitely did not want to get pregnant. She would just have to wait and see what happened.

53

Organising the buying of the giraffe was fairly straight forward, but getting the licenses was a bit of a trial. At last she managed and rang Dick, only to find out from Mobia that Dick was on a safari in Masailand and would not be back until the weekend. Mobia said that he was playing rugby, but that it was a home game. Polly took a chance and organised the darting for Monday morning. She got Gideon to organise the staff. She had already organised the pens to hold them on the ranch and the crates to transport them.

She was frightened to use the veterinary radio call up, as she felt it was not an emergency. She was delighted, when he rang on Friday night. He sounded so pleased to speak to her. He said he thought he would be able to organise the time off on Monday. He said he would go into work tomorrow morning and try, and fix it. Would she like to come out to supper after the Saturday rugby game? Polly said she would love that. She would see him at the game at 'Nondes'.

Polly did a little jig, because she was so pleased. She had a fit of nerves, when she was getting ready to go to 'Nondes'. What should she wear? Should she take an overnight bag? That was certainly too presumptuous. Why had she been so bold before? She had just stripped off in front of him. What did he think of her? Well he would not have asked her, if he had not wanted her to come. He could easily have darted the giraffe, as a purely business arrangement. At last the bold Polly asserted itself. She was sure she needed to look pretty. She put on a mid-calf, floral dress. She just hoped Dick would not think she looked like a flower garden.

Nairobi was quite busy and so as she had to cross the city, she arrived just as the players ran on to the pitch. To her delight, Dick waved to her. She was worried that he would get a ticking off from the captain.

In fact Dick caught the opposition kick-off and there was a horrible crunch as he was tackled. Polly's heart was in her mouth, but he staggered to his feet and ran after the play. In fact it was a very hard game. She was joined by one of the wives called Ruth who had been up in Kitali. Ruth seemed pleased to see her. Ruth teased her saying,

"If 'Nondes' are losing you can always take off your knickers."
Polly answered

"That was so embarrassing. I'm surprised Dick invited me to this game." Ruth replied,

"I'm not. He is always talking about you. Saying how marvellous you are and how you have managed so well in keeping your father's business going. I'm sure he wanted to ask you to a game, but thought you were too busy. Anyhow, I'm very pleased to see you. Some of the older 'Nondes' are pretty stuffy. You are really good fun. You are just what the club needs. Also I think you are just what Dick needs. Before that weekend, I was worried about Dick. He seemed to have lost his way. Also he was working too hard. He seems much more cheerful now."

This was music to Polly's ears, but she said nothing and just smiled.

Actually Polly was pleased, when the game was over. She was just so relieved that Dick was unhurt. He certainly looked exhausted. She could not stop herself and ran to him give him a hug. She was very pleased that he responded so readily. Then he was very apologetic about getting mud on her dress. Polly told him he should not worry. She said she was worried that he would think she looked like a flower garden. He bobbed forward and kissed her left breast through her dress.

"I just wanted to pollinate that flower!"

"Dick you are so naughty."

Then she whispered,

"I hope you will be able to follow my arrow later."

"I hope to kiss what I find at the end of it!"

Polly could not stop herself from blushing,

"Now you have really up scuttled me. Bugger off and get changed!"

Polly had hoped that they would go for supper on their own, but they were sucked into a group. In fact it was good fun. It was not late, when they got back to their Landrovers which were parked near 'Nondes'. The others were then going to take taxis into town to go clubbing. Dick whispered to Polly,

"I don't fancy clubbing do you want to follow me back to my house." Rather breathlessly she replied,

"Yes, I would love that."

So they managed to lose the others and drive in convoy to Lower Kabete. On the drive Polly thought, '*I must not be too forward. It is going to be hard, as I want him so much.*'

As soon as they were in the house all her good intentions were lost and they were soon kissing passionately. Somehow he managed to get his hand inside her bra and he whispered,

"These two beautiful flowers are standing proud to be pollinated."

Polly did not reply, but continued to kiss him. Then with great strength of character she pushed him away from her.

"Dick I have a confession. You may not want to follow the arrow. I am totally wanton. After that lovely weekend in Kitali, I went out and bought some contraceptive pills. Somehow I feel guilty. I am a virgin, but it feels wrong to want you so much."

"Polly, sometimes you do talk a lot of Tommy Rot!"

He swung her into his arms and carried her into his bedroom. He bounced her on to her back on the bed and before she could protest, he pulled her knickers off. With a wicked grin he said,

"It's time to follow the arrow."

She awoke lying in his arms. Their lovemaking had been very energetic. She had expected to be sore, but she felt wonderful. She gave his neck a little kiss and dropped off back to sleep. It was well after 10.00 am when she woke up properly. She sat up and stretched her arms up. Dick smiled up at her. With a big smile she said,

"That was bloody glorious. Having one's virginity taken by an old man with some experience has lots of advantages. I don't feel a bit sore. As he probably has got old-age sight, I suppose it was useful to have an arrow to point him in the right direction. Is he like the bulls and can only be used twice a week? Or could he follow the arrow again?"

That was too much for Dick,

"You cheeky madam!"

He rolled her on to her tummy and got on top of her in one movement. Louise would definitely have agreed that Polly got 'a bit of that'! I think Louise would have been surprised that Polly seemed to be laughing and teasing him during the whole performance, until he did some wicked things with his fingers and Polly buried her face in the pillow to muffle her cries in her ecstasy.

Eventually they got up and had a breakfast at lunchtime before going for a long walk around the Kabete club golf course. They held hands and had ridiculous grins on their faces.

In the evening Dick showed Polly the dart-gun which he had borrowed. He explained that because it was so powerful it was really only suitable for very large thick skinned game animals. He suggested that she might like to get a crossbow which would be suitable for most of the medium, sized plains game. These he said were not that expensive. She could buy some normal bolts to practice with before using the hypodermic bolts. Also he suggested that for smaller plains game she could use a blow-pipe. Dick admitted that he had not had any experience with either of these, but he would definitely be pleased to help her.

Then he started talking about drug dosages. Polly silenced him with a kiss and said, with a giggle,

"How about having a little bit more archery practice before we drive in convoy to my home?"

They were up at dawn. Gideon joined them for breakfast on the veranda. They discussed how they were going to go about the operation. Polly said that she would go with Dick in his Landrover. Gideon would come with Hak in her Landrover and Noah would bring the lorry with the crates and the majority of the staff. Because it was all new there was a holiday feeling. All the staff seemed to be happy.

They reached the ranch with the giraffe in forty minutes. They could see them from the veranda of the farm house. The rancher had experience of a game trapping company before. Apparently they had chased the poor giraffe for over two hours and only managed to lasso it, when it was totally exhausted. The rancher did not want that to happen again. He said he was going to watch from his veranda. Dick was nervous. They took the window off the passenger side door by just undoing two nuts. Gideon drove and Polly sat in the back. Dick sat in the passenger seat.

The giraffe were used to vehicles so that they could get within fifteen yards of the herd quite easily. Gideon selected a male and pointed it out to Dick. Dick had no problem shooting a dart into its rump. The whole herd of approximately twenty animals set off at a canter, but as Gideon did not move the Landrover, they stopped

57

within thirty yards and turned to look back. Polly knew Dick was worried. She stroked the back of his neck. After about ten minutes the giraffe started to stagger. In two more minutes he went down on to his knees and then he went down into lateral recumbency.

Gideon stood on the bonnet of the Landrover and waved his arms. This was the prearranged signal. Hak who had been sitting in the back of the Landrover with Polly stealthily got out. Polly went to follow him, but he indicated with his hand that she should stay put. Polly whispered to Dick,

"Hak is worried about the danger of me being thrown ten feet in the air and landing on my bottom, unlike somebody I know who insisted that I took my clothes off, so he could see if I had got a bruise." She smiled, when she saw him blush.

Hak was soon satisfied that the giraffe was out for the count. They had all got out of the Landrover, as the lorry drove up. Noah backed the lorry up to a termite mound and several of the staff set about digging the top off, and so making a platform. They had brought some thick planks which they made into a ramp. Then they pulled the giraffe on to a tarpaulin. They managed with great difficulty to get the giraffe into one of the crates in the back of the lorry. Dick then gave the giraffe the antidote to the drug which he had put in the dart, into the jugular vein. It was miraculous. In 30 seconds the giraffe staggered to its feet in the crate. Dick was very relieved, as it did not seem to have suffered anything from the anaesthetic or from all the manhandling.

They decided to just get Noah to move the giraffe in the crate a short distance into the shade, as they hoped to be able to load the second giraffe soon. This was not to be. Sadly although Dick hit the rump of the female giraffe that he was aiming for, the dart bounced off. They retrieved the dart and it had injected the drug somewhere, but the animal did not seem to be effected.

Now the giraffe were much more nervous. They continually moved not quite out of range, but a little further away than Dick was happy with. Polly suggested a different approach. She and Hak would go on foot to keep the animals attention, so that Gideon could drive Dick in the Landrover a little nearer. Dick was worried about Polly's safety, but she reassured him that she would be fine. She joked with him, saying,

"If you hit me with a dart, make sure you have your wicked way with me before I die. I think you will have a little time!" Dick looked even more worried after Polly had said that.

Polly and Hak quietly worked their way around the far side of the giraffe. Polly had always been fond of Hak. She had many happy memories of going with him to learn what her father called 'bush craft'. Polly had no fear, when she was with Hak. She just knew that, if she did as he instructed that she would come to no harm.

When Hak considered that they were in the correct position they moved in line abreast towards the giraffe. They moved slowly. The giraffe became aware of them. They became a bigger threat than the Landrover. The giraffe watched them. They moved their ears more, as they got agitated. Hak did not want to spook them, so he indicated to Polly to stop. The giraffe just watched them from their great height. They turned and walked sedately towards the Landrover. Polly thought she and Hak would follow them, but Hak indicated that she should continue to stand. The giraffe continued to amble. Hak was obviously gauging the best distance for Dick's shot.

He indicated to Polly to start walking again. Almost immediately the giraffe stopped and studied them. Polly knew then that they would be presenting their rumps towards the Landrover.

Suddenly it all happened. The giraffe took off at a canter to Polly's left. Then she heard the shot. It was not really a shot more like a pop. To Polly it was almost like magic. Hak was right beside her. She was in no danger. Hak indicated that they should just standstill and let the giraffe go. They could hear the noise of the Landrover starting and slowly going through the bush to their left. When it was past them they both started to walk purposely to where Hak obviously thought the giraffe would stop.

Probably, as the giraffe were more alert and therefore more resistant to the drug, or because the drug had not been injected into the very best place in the muscle, the female took considerably longer to collapse than the male. Gideon realised that they could not see Noah in the lorry. Nor could he see them. Having dropped Dick with the giraffe he drove as fast as he could back to Noah. Hearing this Hak and Polly started to run to Dick. He was very relieved to see them. Polly said,

"Shall I sit on its neck?" He replied,

"Don't you bloody dare?" She laughed,

"Oh, so now you have seen my bare bottom, you are not bothered about seeing it again to inspect it to check for any bruising. How quickly romance dies!" Dick was speechless.

There was nothing really for them to do until the lorry arrived. Dick hoped it would arrive before the giraffe started to wake up. Hak started to clear the bush in a good spot for the giraffe to be loaded.

It was not long before Noah arrived. Then they all set to and loaded the second animal. Dick gave it the antidote and it was soon up. They drove slowly in convoy back to the ranch and the enclosures which they had prepared. The giraffe could see each other over a high fence, but they could not kick or fight. Polly would have loved to know what they thought of each other. Was the female like her, very wanton! Then she smiled to herself. She was only wanton as far as Dick was concerned. She was not wanton with Roly!

Polly was really looking forward to making friends with both of the giraffe. They looked so beautiful with their enormous, languid eyes.

It was tea time before they had unloaded the animals. Polly was delighted that Dick did not need much persuading to say the night. Josiah made them a good supper, while they had showers. Polly suggested that Dick had the first shower, as she said that she would take longer. Then she crept up behind him in the shower. Much to her delight, he nearly jumped out of his skin. Their combined shower was great fun.

They had an early breakfast so that Dick was not held up by the traffic. Polly teased him that he was so conscientious. Secretly she was delighted. She realised the work ethic had been very deeply ingrained in her at 'Norwich High School'. Polly was sad that she would not be seeing him for some time, as he had to go on a ten day government safari. She had however plenty to do. She needed to source a dart gun as it was not fair to borrow one all the time. She also wanted to buy a crossbow and a blow pipe. She knew she would have to practice with them, as she planned that she was going to be a hunter as well as Gideon.

Buying the crossbow was easy as they were readily available in Nairobi. The blowpipe had to be ordered from the UK, as did the hypodermic darts for both weapons. Polly laughed at herself. She was so impatient. She had not got any orders yet!

Polly was pleased that she found shooting the crossbow quite easy. It had a telescopic sight, but it was not heavy. Also it did not have a kick. It did not hurt her shoulder. When she fired her shotgun or one of the bigger rifles she had to wear quite a lot of quilted clothes, so that she did not get a sore shoulder. These were hot. She could fire the crossbow wearing a top or even her bikini.

She imagined that she would need a large amount of puff for the blowpipe. She started to do exercises. She remembered how the girls at school who wanted to make their boobs bigger used to exercise to the chant of 'I must, I must improve my bust!'

Polly liked her bust. She thought her breasts were just right. She looked very feminine, but she did not have, nor would she have wanted big boobs. She was dying to ask Dick whether he liked her boobs. She knew he liked her legs, as he often said so. She also knew he liked her bottom, because he rarely missed a chance to fondle it.

So she was kept busy during the day, it was just in bed, when she really missed him. She so loved his big arms around her. She also had to admit she really enjoyed, in Louise's words, 'a bit of that'!

On the Friday evening after she had finished her early supper, she suddenly felt very naughty. She was just in a towelling robe as normally she would go to bed. She put on her sexiest underwear, a low top and a short skirt. She got in the Landrover and drove to Dick's house at Kabete. She was very excited and then suddenly became nervous. What if he brought another girl home? What if he had friends around to dinner? She would look a right trollop. She very nearly turned around. However she didn't. It was dark, when she got to his house. There was only the porch light on. She panicked. Had he had an accident? Then she saw Mobia in the headlights. She called to him in Kikuyu,

"Is everything alright? Surely Dick should be home?" Mobia replied,

"Yes, I am a little worried. He should be home. I have some food ready for him. Would you like some? I am sure there is enough."

"Don't worry, Mobia. I have already eaten. Hopefully he will be home soon. I would love a cup of coffee."

Polly came in. She sat in an easy chair in the sitting room. Dick was still not home at 10.00 pm. Mobia came in. He said normally, if Dick was this late, he put his dinner in the fridge and went to bed. With a chuckle he suggested Polly also went to bed. She blushed and said she would do just that.

Initially she was a little shy and just lay on the bed in her clothes. Then she thought this stupid. She got up and took her skirt and top off and got into bed. Although she was worried she was also tired. She soon went to sleep.

It was 2.00 am, when Dick got home. The rear half-shaft in the Landrover had sheared off. He could still drive the vehicle in four wheel drive except going up hills, when he had to go in reverse as the front wheels would not grip well enough. His spirits lifted, when he recognised Polly's Landrover. He did not bother to unpack the Landrover. He crept in and saw Polly asleep in his bed. He realised how dirty he was, when he smelt her gentle fragrance. He crept in to the spare room and had a good shower. Then he came into his bedroom. He left the light on, as he knew if he turned it off she would wake. He slipped naked into bed. She did not wake, but rolled towards him and buried her face in his chest. He gently put his arms around her. They both slept. At dawn Polly woke. She knew instantly, where she was. She kissed his chest and then went back to sleep totally relaxed, now that she knew he was safe.

They woke together about an hour later. Poly kissed him gently and murmured.

"I was worried about you and I should not admit it, but I was desperate for these strong arms to be around me. I came round after supper last night. What happened?"

"I had a breakdown. It was a lovely surprise to find you, when I got in at 2.00 am." His hand fondled her bottom through her silk knickers. "Does this sexy underwear keep you warm, when you are alone in bed?"

"Of course it doesn't, you numpty, it was put on especially for you. Initially I felt shy and lay on the bed fully clothed. Then I got braver and took my skirt and top off, and got into bed. What I would really like is a pair of big gentle hands to take my bra and knickers off. What you do after that is up to you."

Dick needed no further encouragement. However he was very gentle and slowly caressed her. Polly felt really loved. When they both calmed down, she asked,

"Do you like my boobs?" Dick did not answer, but just kissed them and then said,

"What a strange thing to ask. I think they are lovely. They are just right. They are two lovely handfuls." Polly laughed,

"You have got enormous hands. I don't think they are that big. I was asking because I have started to do specific exercises to improve my lung capacity for using the blowpipe which I have ordered. It made me chuckle, as I remembered girls at school chanting, 'I must, I must improve my bust'."

"Well I think your bust is lovely and it certainly does not need any improvement."

Dick started to suck her nipples quite vigorously. They ended up making love again.

Polly stayed at his house for the rest of the weekend. She rang Josiah so that he knew where she was. When she returned to the ranch early on Monday morning she was very pleased, as she was sure the giraffe were pleased to see her. Later in the day she was absolutely delighted, as she received a cable from a zoo in Japan requesting a large consignment of antelope. These were all native to East Africa, but some were really rare. Catching them would be a real challenge. It was just what she had hoped for, as it would give a large amount of work for all the staff. She could charge a very large fee which would pay their wages and would make Roly happy, as she could fulfil his financial plan. She would not have to touch her secret stash of foreign currency in the bank with her mother's jewellery. She had rather burnt her boats regarding selling her body! Was she now rather second hand? She didn't see it that way. She loved Dick. She knew he was not just a father figure. She knew he loved her which gave her a large amount of confidence.

She knew she would have to work hard completing all the paperwork for the Game Department. She laughed at herself, as she knew so many girls of her age would have paid someone to do the work, so that they could have time going to parties and sunbathing. That was not her way. She got a large amount of satisfaction in working hard. She just hoped no disaster occurred, such as an outbreak of Foot and Mouth Disease (FMD), so that the shipment was delayed and ate into her profits.

In the same way that she enjoyed hard profitable work, so did all the staff. They had all worked with her father for many years. They had watched her grow up. It seemed miraculous that they accepted her as their leader. She was still in her teens. They all looked to her and yet they were very protective of her. She could not help laughing at herself. She had been worried about her boobs. Now she had Dick's reassurance that he liked them. She was sure he would still like them when they were all large and swollen, and there was a little Dick greedily sucking them. She reached for another biscuit with her coffee, but stopped herself. She did not want a fat tummy or a big bottom regardless of what Dick or Josiah wanted!

Chapter 7

Polly gets to grips with darting

There was a hive of activity at the ranch. Not only did they have to construct all the pens, but also they had to construct the small crates to transport the animals after capture. These same crates would be used to transport the animals on the train, when they went down to Mombasa to go on the boat to Japan. The Japanese would have to pay for these crates. Polly could feel the happy atmosphere at the ranch. She felt happy as well.

She had been thinking about shooting the crossbow. When she had been practicing she had noticed that, when she could rest her arms on something, she was much more accurate, than when she had to hold the bow up. It was not that heavy, but it was very cumbersome. She thought she could have a mattress on the top of the roof-rack on the long wheel-base safari Landrover. Then she could lie on the top. She would then have a good platform to rest her arms before shooting. She realised that she would need some straps, to strap her to the mattress so that she did not get bounced off, when they were following the game. She went to see Zeb who was one of the skinners. She had seen how he had done some really good leather work. He said he would be delighted to make her a harness.

The following Friday it was finished. Polly thought it would work very well. Then she had some very naughty thoughts. She rang up Dick. She knew he would not be home, but she knew Mobia would be likely to know what he was up to. Mobia said he was working down at Naivasha. Polly knew that was only fifty miles away. Mobia added that Dick had said he was going to play squash with a friend of his and that the friend said his wife would make supper for him.

Polly made a plan she told Mobia that she would come over after supper, as she had got a surprise for Dick. She said there would be no need for Mobia to wait up. Mobia chuckled and told her that Dick had been so delighted, when she had come over before uninvited. Dick had told Mobia that he wanted to invite Polly over, but he did not like to, as he knew how busy she was with the game capture business.

Polly worked hard on Friday. She even managed a long-winded visit to the Game Department to get the permits. They were planning to start the capture on Monday.

After her supper she had a shower and put on a sexy shortie nighty under her shirt and skirt. Then she drove to Dick's house. Mobia with a big grin let her in and told her that he would go to bed, but he would make them a big breakfast in the morning.

Polly went into Dick's bedroom. She had brought the straps that Zeb had made. She did not feel shy tonight, particularly after what Mobia had told her. She wondered if Kenyans were more open with her, as she spoke to them in their tribal languages.

She pretended that Dick's bed was the mattress on to top of the Landrover. Making sure she had a book to read she took off her clothes, leaving her, just in her nighty. She experimented with the straps. Zeb had made them so that there was a loop over the top of each thigh and another strap over her waist. The idea was that she would be shooting on her tummy with her elbows steadying the cross bow.

Dick had a big eiderdown which she was going to pull over her so that she was not cold. She strapped her thighs down, but before she strapped her waist down she gave a little wiggle. This made her nighty ride up on to her bottom.

She settled down with her book, to wait. It was just like sunbathing on her tummy. She could never just sunbathe, she always had a book. Eventually she heard Dick's Landrover. She knew he would have seen hers. She thought he would expect her to be in the living room sitting up waiting for him. She pushed the book under the pillow. She pulled the eiderdown off and gave a sexy wiggle. She felt her nighty ride up, as she had planned.

Dick came in roaring with laughter. He put his hand on her bottom and gave it a gentle squeeze. Then he kissed the back of her neck. Polly whispered,

"I came to ask your advice about this arrangement for my crossbow shooting from the top of the Landrover." He chuckled,

"This needs some very careful consideration." He ran a hand up inside her thighs,

"Yes I think those legs are wide enough to give you a firm stance, as if you were shooting. Now let's see if the waist belt is tight enough so there is just the right amount of movement."

All the time he had one hand between her legs. It was not long before Polly had to bury her face in his pillow, to stop crying out. She bit into the pillow as she felt him enter her. Her mind flashed back to the bulls at the AI Centre. It felt so good. She didn't mind if Dick had a smug look on his face, as he came deep inside her. She sighed with a lovely feeling of fulfilment. She was even excited again as Dick gently undid the straps so that she could wriggle on top of him. They both slept.

It had not been late, when Dick had come in on the previous night, so they were both up in good time for Mobia's promised breakfast. Then Dick had to be her tutor. She needed to know the dosages of the various medicines which he had purchased for her to dart the antelope. He then set off to work after she had given him a big kiss.

"Good luck with the game today. Could I persuade you to come to my house tonight? You can come as late as you like." Then she added with a cheeky grin,

"If I feel like running away, I will strap myself to the top of the Landrover. You seemed to rather like that."

Dick just went very red,

"You are so bloody sexy. I don't know how I'm going to concentrate at the office. Take care, My Darling." Those two words were etched into Polly's brain.

Dick was not late that evening. He just ate the sausage, mash and bake-beans. Then he slipped out. He did not want to get a lot of ribbing from the rest of the team. He was so early that Polly had only just come in. She was delighted to see him. He sat with her as she ate her supper which Josiah had prepared. He told her about the game. They laughed together about him slipping off. Then suddenly Polly felt guilty.

"I hope I don't embarrass you too much. I don't want you rushing off and leaving your friends."

"I wanted to rush off and be with you. I understand how hard you are working." He took her face in his big rough hands and kissed her gently on the lips.

67

"We both have busy lives. I treasure every moment that I can be with you. Of course you don't embarrass me. The rest of the team and their wives or girl friends are always asking about you."

Polly found that very reassuring. She wondered if it was possible to love someone too much. After supper she had a quick shower and then sat on his knee in her towel dressing gown. They chatted on. She loved the feel of his naughty hand which slipped inside her robe. She was glad she didn't have any pants on. She gave a deep sigh,

"Let's go out in the moonlight and check on the giraffe. I usually say goodnight to them before I go to bed. They are getting so tame, I'm sure you won't spook them. Hopefully next time you come I will have some other species to show you."

She wrapped her robe around her, as she put on a pair of flip-flops. Holding hands they walked out into the yard. The night watchman greeted them. The way he gave a slight bow of his head was not missed by Dick. He knew how devoted all the staff were to her. It was not just because she talked to them in their own languages it was also with a genuine respect. He remembered when she was just an eight year old how the staff all loved her. He wondered if it was because there was no lady of the house. However he knew of many Kenyan matrons who did not have half the respect of their staff that Polly had. He thought it was because she genuinely was one of them. They knew she would do all in her power to help them.

Polly had been correct. The giraffe were pleased to see her and they were not concerned by Dick's presence. He loved it that she had such a wonderful, gentle way with animals. He knew he also had what farmers called a 'way with livestock'. He put his arm around her shoulders,

"Polly will you marry me? I want you to have my children." She stiffened. Dick thought that she was going to reject him. She turned, her robe fell open. She wrapped her arms around him. She kissed him passionately. Then she broke away from him.

"I guess that kiss answers your question. I would love to marry you Dick and have your children. I was only thinking a day or two ago that I bet any of your offspring will be greedy little sods and play havoc with my tits. Make the most of them now. I bet they won't fit in to your hands for long."

Dick chuckled with pleasure and if he was honest with relief that she had not rejected him,

"You don't mind that I am so much older than you?"

"Of course, I don't mind." He could see her cheeky smile in the moonlight.

"When we are married, I will restrict you to sex once a month. I imagine you will be up to that OK."

Dick laughed.

"I will get Zeb to make some straps to hold you down, so I can have my wicked way with you when ever I want." Polly hugged him to her, whispering,

"Promises, promises. Come on let's go to bed. I'm going to have MY WICKED way with you right now."

They certainly had a night to remember. Josiah could remember, when he was young. He only made breakfast, when he knew they were up.

Dick spent the whole day with Polly on the ranch on Sunday. They were both sad that he had to go home to get his Landrover all loaded up, as he had to leave to go on safari at 5.00 am on Monday morning. Just as they were kissing goodbye, Polly said,

"I'm coming with you in convoy. I can help you get ready. We can then cuddle up for the night. I will get up early with you in the morning."

That's what they did. They were in bed before 11.00 pm. They both knew they would not get to sleep easily unless they made love. They then slept like logs. When they hugged in the morning, Dick felt really guilty that he had not got a ring. Polly said to cheer him up and tease him,

"I'm not worried about a ring. I am worried to know what I am going to do with all the cattle you will be sending across for my bride price!"

She pushed him into the Landrover and they both set off in different directions. They did not meet again until Dick arrived at Polly's home ten days later. He had managed to complete all his work on the Thursday so he had driven through the night and arrived at her home soon after 2.00 am. She woke, when she heard a vehicle. She ran out in a kikoi, when she saw it was him. The night watchman smiled, as she dragged Dick into the house. He saw them making love on the floor in the living room. They did not have time to get to the bedroom.

After a late breakfast on Friday morning, they went into Nairobi. Polly was embarrassed by how much Dick had insisted on paying for the ring. She thought it was lovely. It flashed in the sunlight. After lunch Dick had to go and clock in at Kabete. They agreed that they would meet at the rugby game on Saturday.

Polly made sure she was not late. She saw Ruth on the touch line and went, and joined her. Ruth immediately saw her ring. She gave Polly a hug,

"I knew he was the right man for you. I'm glad for you both. He has got more sense than I would have credited him with. So many of these men can't make up their minds, they string young girls along. The girls get fed up and go to the UK. The men moon around moaning that the girl has walked out on them. Not Dick. He said all the time after that Kitali weekend, what a marvellous girl you were and now he has bought you a ring. When are you going to get married?" Polly answered,

"I'm not sure. We have not really discussed it. Both of our parents have died, so it is really up to us. I think we both would like to get married as soon as possible. I would love to get pregnant. I'm so keen to have his children."

"Good for you. I am so pleased to hear you say that. We had our two when we were really quite young. I've never regretted it. Don't get me wrong, but I will be delighted, when our two boys are off our hands. We will still be young and have some fun together as a couple. If you leave it until you are older, you are then too old, when they are grown up to enjoy yourselves." Polly laughed,

"I remember laughing with Gideon my right hand man on the day of my Dads funeral eighteen months ago. I remember saying to him that I felt very young at eighteen, but then I said to him that if I had been a wife of his that I would have probably have had three children by my age and my tits would hang down to my waist. I hope they won't!"

"Oh Polly, you are so funny. They are bound to droop a bit. Even if you didn't have any children, they would. They don't have to droop too much. You have got a lovely trim figure. You will just have to make sure Dick massages them a lot."

"He will enjoy doing that!" She added,

"I also will enjoy him doing it!"

They did not say any more as the game started and there were more spectators. It was only at halftime that Louise came up. Polly showed her the ring. Louise gave a great Whoop. She called some of the other girls over, before saying,

"That is wonderful news. I was so worried about you up at Kitali. Dick is almost twice your age and I was worried that he was taking advantage of you. It seems as if you knew exactly what you were doing."

"Louise, you make me sound so calculating. We love each other. In fact I think I have loved Dick since I was eight years old. I never thought he would ask me to marry him. You make it sound, as if I slept with him to trap him. I'm not pregnant. I would be mortified if you thought I was that sort of a girl."

Louise was all contrite then.

"I didn't mean you were on the lookout for a husband. It was just that you were so confident. I was just worried that you were really naïve. I'm so please for you both."

The game had got really exciting so they both watched in silence. Polly thought, '*I know he loves his rugby. I don't want him to stop because of me, but I do so worry about him. He seems so totally exhausted after the games. The others do not seem quite so tired. I don't think it is really his age, although he is one of the eldest. I think that the main problem is that he is away so much on safari that he does not get to training. I'm not going to say anything, but I'm going to make sure that I come to his home rather than let him drive over to my home all the time.*'

Although Polly did not know much about rugby, she could see that Dick was a key player. He was in the thick of it. He really gave his all. She was very proud of him and kept cheering. She was so pleased at the end of the game that they had won. She ran to him and wrapped her arms around him. She knew he was pleased, as he didn't speak, but held her very close. She said,

"Well played, My Darling. That was a great win."

She kissed him on the lips. As they broke apart, he managed to say,

"You are such a wonderful girl I feel stronger than ever now."

They walked towards the clubhouse holding hands. Dick said,

"I don't care how much ribbing I get. I don't care who knows how much I love you. I can't wait to marry you."

That night they slept at Dick's house. They both had drunk quite a bit, as they had been made to celebrate their engagement by Dick's team mates. Polly was just grateful that they all seemed to accept her. Dick got into bed first and Polly wriggled in on top of him. She kissed him passionately and felt him hard under her. She whispered,

"I thought you might be too tired. Do you remember that morning at Kitali when Louise crept through our room and I called out, Oh Dick you are so big. You really feel big now."

She pushed him inside her. Whether it was because she loved him so much or because she had been longing for this moment since the morning before, but her hormones seemed to go mad. She thrust down on to him and had a massive orgasm and nearly bit him in ecstasy. She groaned, as she felt him come inside her. He hugged her to him and they were not sure if they had passed out or slept. They did not wake until the early hours when they gently made love again.

They had a lovely quiet day together on the Sunday. They went for a walk in the afternoon around Lower Kabete. They had an early supper and then with a heavy heart Polly had to leave him. She had planned to start capturing the antelope at dawn in the morning. She knew Gideon would have everything prepared. She did not want to let him down.

Chapter 8

Dick goes on safari to make a
new stock route.

Dick also planned to leave to go on safari at day break. He was going to make a new stock route from Galole on the Tana River through the country of the Orma, to Galana Ranch on the Sabaki River. Galana Ranch had plans to make a causeway across the Sabaki River and a stock route beside Tsavo East National Park to the Mombasa/Nairobi Railway at Mackinnon Road.

He set off in a Government Landrover with an efficient driver called Mbaruk. Mbaruk had everything well organised. He had spare fuel in four Jerry Cans. He also had several Local Purchase Orders (LPOs) to purchase more fuel on the journey. Dick had all his usually camping gear with a lot of extra water, as he knew that once they left the Tana River, there would be no more water until they reached the Sabaki River.

Behind them was a Bedford 4 X 4 driven by Pius. Pius was always happy, nothing upset him. In the lorry were ten 44 gallon drums of white wash. These were for making enormous marks on the ground so that the stock route could be seen from the air. The idea was for the Veterinary Department to fly a very elderly water engineer who could not possibly make the arduous journey by road, down the stock route. The engineer could then make suggestions for sighting water holes and catchment pans in this very dry area.

Also in the lorry were a gang of men who were going to clear the bush so that they could, not only make the marks on the ground, but also that they could continue on a direct compass bearing. The bush was very variable. In places it was very thick, but mainly it was sparse. There were very few trees to help with navigation. There were only two low hills in the whole area. Dick had two major problems; water and navigation.

Having set off early, they made good time and reached Galole before night fall. They all camped in the Government Compound. The following morning, after they had filled up with fuel and water, they set off on a compass bearing due south from the main Garissa to Garsen Road opposite the turn off North to Galole. The going was much rougher than Dick had imagined. He was very glad that Mbaruk was driving. Mbaruk was very careful and drove slowly so that they did not crash down into each hole in the surface. It should be remembered that they were driving in virgin bush. They dare not deviate from the compass baring. Dick stuck this for about half an hour. Then he called a halt. He thought they had hardly gone more than a mile. They could still hear the traffic on the main Garissa to Garsen Road.

They all got off the lorry and had a discussion to try to find an easier way to travel on a compass bearing. It was Mbaruk who suggested that the lorry should lead. Dick should stand on one of the drums of white wash and take the compass bearing and carefully remember which tree they were aiming for. Then they would continue on this heading with everyone helping with the bush clearing. It was very laborious and time consuming, but at least they all felt they were moving in the correct direction.

It was half way through the afternoon when they came to an open place with a sandy surface. Dick thought this was too near to be a suitable place for a watering point, for the stock route, as the Landrover's speedometer only showed eight miles. However there were two trees and so it was a good place to camp. Dick called a halt. Everyone was hot and tired.

In the morning, to be on the safe side they made a big letter A which could be seen from the air. Then they set off again. The bush was still quite thick and so they made slow, but sure, progress. They stopped for a half hour break at noon. Dick was grateful to them all, for keeping going on this arduous task. He did not want to impose on their goodwill. He could feel the camaraderie developing. He was pleased that he had stopped, as they did not come to a suitable place to camp until 5.30 pm. It was too small a sandy area to be suitable for a water point. However Dick had no idea what the terrain was like even a 100 yards away, let alone two miles away, so they made a

B mark to be visible from the air. The speedometer showed they had travelled eleven miles.

The overall plan was to have watering points at approximately twenty five mile intervals. This was the distance a mob of cattle could travel without water. This was far from ideal and it was hoped that they could have watering points eventually at approximately twelve and a half mile intervals.

Water was the key to trekking cattle. When water points had been established, further infrastructure would be established. Thorn bomas would be constructed and huts made for the herders. Long cattle races would be required so that the cattle could have veterinary treatments. Eventually either cattle dips or spray races would be built. These could be used by the local Orma people over whose land the stock was being trekked. The Orma chiefs had agreed for the stock route, not only for these benefits, but also because the Government, through the Veterinary Department's Livestock Marketing Division, were buying the surplus cattle. This reduced the over grazing and provided cash for the local people.

The following day was even worse, as the bush was thicker. They only managed eight miles, but at least they stopped on an open area at a reasonable time in the afternoon, so everyone could relax in the day light, after they had made the large C mark.

Dick's team seemed to be very happy. They could see that the task and the safari were going to continue longer than had been planned. They all received extra safari allowance which nearly doubled their pay. Also because they were on safari in this remote area they accrued more leave. It was only Dick who was unhappy. He was really missing Polly. His only consolation was that he had been very sensible in asking her to marry him. They had a whole life time ahead of them together. He had a job to do and he must get on and do it.

He was wise enough to know that it was vital he did not push his team too hard. They were in very hot dry country. Just travelling was very hard work, apart from the entire bush clearing task which was extremely hard work. Dick made sure he did his share. It made him smile, as at least it was keeping him fit for rugby.

The following morning they arrived at what initially looked like a totally impassable dry river bed. They stopped and two pairs of men set out in opposite directions to see if there was an easier place to cross. Dick gave them strict instructions that they were to carry sufficient water and make marks on the small acacia trees so that they would not get lost. He also suggested that they only proceeded for a thousand paces. If they did not find a suitable crossing point, they were to return. In the meantime Dick and the rest of the team started clear the bush at the site, as Dick knew that the eventual stock route would come to this point. It was very hard work. They managed to clear the bush to the edge of the dry river bed, before the first pair returned. They had no news of any better site. Twenty minutes later the other pair returned. They had similar bad news.

There was a drop of twelve feet from the edge of the soil down to the sand of the river bed. The bottom was twenty paces wide before there was a similar bank on the other side. The two sides were not really banks, but small cliffs of soil which had been cut through by water one rainy season years before. This actual area, only normally received, about two inches of rain each year which fell in one down pour in April or May. Occasionally there might be a similar down pour in November, but that was not every year.

There was nothing to it, but they would have to dig away the banks. At least they could just shovel the soil into the dry river bed. This would help to build up a causeway. It took them two hard days. Dick sent the two drivers back in the lorry to get more water and food, as he now knew they were going to need it, unless the going radically improved. He also told them to send back word on the radio at Galole to tell Kabete his difficulties. He also asked the Veterinary Department to get word, if possible, to Polly.

When they eventually set off from the other side of the donga the mood of the whole team was very upbeat. There hopes were dashed, as they came to another donga within four miles. The donga was not so wide, as the last one, nor were the banks so tall, but they had another serious problem. When they had cleared a small path Mbaruk took Dick through in the Landrover to scout up ahead to see if there were more dongas. Mercifully the ground was more open and there were no deep dongas. Mbaruk and Dick were just turning round, when they heard the lorry, so they stopped, thinking the lorry would soon get to them.

They were standing chatting, when the whole team came running towards them shouting,

"Bees, Bees."

Mbaruk with great presence of mind jumped into the Landrover and set off and managed to get about a quarter of a mile further on. Dick turned and ran with the team. They had out run the bees. Most of the men had been stung several times. Pius had fared the worst as the bees had invaded the cab of the lorry. He stripped off all his clothes to make sure there were no bees still alive in them. He swore he was never going back to the lorry until all the bees were dead.

Dick now had to summon up his courage. He found his old, safari, bread-oven, made out of an old rectangular aviation fuel can, in the Landrover. He got one of the men to light a small fire inside it. He borrowed clothes from them all to make himself some padding to completely cover his body. He just left a slit for his eyes. Mbaruk checked him over to make sure there were no holes in his defences. Then they put some water on fire to make smoke.

With great trepidation Dick carried the fire pot in his gloved hand back to the lorry. The lorry was still running, where Pius had left it. He had been just coming up out of the dry river bed. It must have hit the bee's nest in a tree, as it started to climb. The cab was surrounded by very angry bees. Dick kept going and pushed the smoking fire pot into the cab. He wound up the window and slammed the door. He went to the other door and got into the smoke filled cab and wound the second window up. The cab was full of bees, but the smoke had quietened them. Coughing and spluttering he systematically started killing the sleepy bees. One got in an eye slit and stung him on his eyebrow. He steadily killed them. The cab was still surrounded by angry flying bees.

At last, when he thought he was going to be sick from coughing, he decided to have a go at moving the lorry. It was already in four wheel drive, so he put his foot on the clutch and put it into first gear. He was off. The fire pot still smoked on the seat beside him. With the engine roaring he climbed the steep side of the donga. For one dreadful moment the wheels spun and he thought he was not going to make it, but then they gripped and he bounced on to the flat surface. As he drove towards the Landrover the numbers of bees flying round the cab rapidly diminished. Mbaruk moved the Landrover and the rest of the staff walked so that eventually Dick could stop. He opened the door and breathed fresh air. It was beautiful.

It took them some time to get sorted out. Then they continued on their trek. Luckily they came to a good camping spot in the middle of the afternoon, so Dick could call a halt. They were all exhausted with the heat and the exertion. It had become very humid and it certainly felt like rain, although it was later in the year than normal. Dick managed to shoot four yellow-necked francolin which they all enjoyed a little of, having roasted them on the fire. It was the smell of the roasting meat which was so tantalising.

Sadly they were not very well prepared around the camp as they were all so used to the dry conditions. That night the rain came in earnest. It rained continuously all night, all the following day and only stopped about an hour before dawn on the next night. Dick had been measuring the amount in a saucepan and he was certain that it was more than fourteen inches.

The camp was pretty miserable during the rain. They were all relieved they had picked a sandy place as the surrounding soil was a quagmire. When the sun eventually returned, their spirits lifted. There was a wonderful smell from the grateful earth. It was miraculous as everywhere had a green sheen. It seemed to arrive within hours. The earth steamed. There were a multitude of butterflies of beautiful colours, mainly blues and whites.

In the middle of the morning they had completed the majority of the drying out of all the tents and equipment. They packed up and started on the trek. Dick just hoped that their large white letters had survived.

They made good progress until the middle of the afternoon, when they were on the lookout for a sandy camping spot. The texture of the soil changed. Mbaruk in the Landrover recognised it. He stopped and flashed his lights. Then he blasted on the horn. Dick heard and beat on the top of the cab of the lorry. Pius stopped. The lorry was beginning to sink. Dick shouted to him,

"Back up. We are in Black Cotton Soil."

Pius reversed. Luckily the Bedford had four-wheel drive. The wheels slipped initially, but then they held. Pius backed up keeping in his original tracks. It was easier for Mbaruk as he was in a smaller vehicle, so he reversed as well. Neither of them tried to turn, until they had reached firmer ground. They were now on normal soil and both vehicles stopped.

Dick was very conscious that it would be very easy for any of the team to get lost. They went out in teams always blazing the trees as they progressed so they could find their way back to this spot. Eventually when they had all returned they discussed what they had discovered.

The good news was that one team had found a very good camping spot on sandy ground just over a mile from their track, in an easterly direction. Dick drew a crude map marking the extent of the Black Cotton Soil, the sand dongas and any other features which they all thought were relevant. They then marked the spot where they were with a big letter D, before moving the mile to a decent camping ground.

What Dick did not know was that the very heavy rain was, not only local in Tana River District, but also had occurred on Mount Kenya. When they got up in the morning they were on a small sand island surrounded by water to various depths. The dongas were really deep. They were fast flowing and the levels were well over the height of a man. It had been so lucky that they had moved to this slightly higher piece of ground. They were now stranded by impassable dongas and the equally impassable glutinous, bottomless, Black Cotton Soil.

They were not unduly concerned as they had plenty of basic food and drinking water. They obviously had plenty of water to wash with. Soon the sun was hot, as normal, so they could collect firewood and it was soon dry. Dick tried to supplement their diet by shooting some Guinea fowl. He shot several yellow-necked francolins most days, as they were very plentiful. One day he even shot a goose.

Dick was worried about Polly. He wondered if her house and the small ranch had been affected by the rainstorms. He knew that it was set on high ground and therefore he thought flooding was unlikely. He hoped the game catching was going according to plan.

Chapter 9

Capturing small antelope

Because Dick was away, Polly was working even harder than normal. She practiced with the crossbow daily. Every time she strapped herself to the mattress on top of the Landrover she thought of Dick. She would wiggle her bottom and wish he was on top of her.

She kept up, doing her upper-body exercises, chanting, "I must I must improve my bust." It always brought a smile to her face. She was looking forward to the arrival of the blow-pipe. In the evenings she would go over the drug dosages, so that she knew them by heart. She hoped she would then, be quicker at preparing the hypodermic darts. Obviously the first dart could be prepared after the victim had been selected, but she did not want to load darts unnecessarily. If she missed or the dart mechanism malfunctioned, she would have to load a replacement in a hurry.

Polly was going to use the crossbow for the medium sized antelope. She had decided to start with Impala which she could capture locally. These were generally found in reasonably large herds of hornless females with one large male which had beautiful lyre shaped horns. She hoped capturing a female would not be difficult. She did not want to cause too much distress and so was reluctant to try to capture the single male. Instead she planned to capture a less mature male. These were found in all male groups. He was going to be her first victim.

She set off strapped to the mattress, Gideon drove and Hak was in the passenger seat. The all male group of Impala showed very little fear of the Landrover. This allowed Gideon to drive up to them, so that Polly had a very easy shot. She hit the Impala in the rump and the dart with its small barb stayed in place. The animal jumped forward on impact of the dart and the rest of the group followed him, but they very soon stopped. Gideon did not move the Landrover, as he could see the whole group.

One of the improvements they had instituted after the giraffe capture was to get small two-way radios. Hak alerted Noah in the lorry. He was not far away and they could hear him start up.

Within five minutes the Impala started to stagger. Hak, wisely, stayed in the Landrover, but gave Noah an update on the situation. When it went down, having summons Noah, Hak and Gideon ran to the animal. Polly had unstrapped herself and was close behind. They quickly secured the Impala and Polly put on a small blind fold. Polly cut out the dart carefully with a scalpel and dressed the small wound with gentian violet. It was an easy task to load it into the crate in the lorry.

Polly was nervous then. She wished Dick was with her. She had to give the antidote intravenously. It was all prepared in a syringe, but it was getting the needle into the jugular that she was concerned about. All the hunting training then came in useful. She steadied herself, Hak who was always mindful for her safety held the horns, Gideon raised the vein with a small noose of thin rope, and Polly had no problem putting the needle into the vein. There was a good flow of blood. She attached the syringe and injected the antidote. Hak removed the blindfold and they all clambered out of the crate. The Impala was up in under half a minute and did not look any worse for his experience.

The whole crew were smiling. They broke into laughs when Gideon stammered,

"Well done Ms Polly." She put her arm around him, saying,

"Thank you Mr Gideon. At least you didn't call me Mr. Dick. That would have made me really cross. It's POLLY."

The darting of the female was equally as quick and successful. Polly had been worried that the herd male might have been more wary and led his females away from the Landrover. However her worries were unfounded.

Noah drove their captives back to their ranch, where their living pens were waiting. Polly and Gideon called into the owner of the ranch who was amazed that they had been so quick. He was really happy for them to return that day to try to capture a pair of Grant's gazelle.

Grant's gazelle also have lyre shaped horns, but unlike Impala they are carried by both sexes. They are fawn, not as red as Impala, nor as large. They rarely are longer than two and a half feet. Polly was worried that they were two small for the crossbow dart. She knew she would have to place the shot more accurately. They definitely had a smaller rump. Once again her hunting experience helped her.

They singled out a female and the whole operation went like clockwork. The male took longer, as the small group were slightly more nervous, when they were approached for the second time. However, Polly's shooting was spot on. She was so pleased to be able to give them the antidote. All the killing had certainly upset her. However she knew that, if she had to shoot an antelope for the pot, she would do it. It was just shooting for trophies which sickened her.

Because of Polly's fear of hurting the smaller antelope with the dart, they decided to wait for the blowpipe for capturing these smaller animals. So they set their sights on some of the larger species. Both the Common Waterbuck and Defassa's Waterbuck were common in their area. They are both similar with quite thick hairy coats. They both are greyish-brown, but are distinguished by the much larger white patch on the rump of the Defassa's Waterbuck.

Capturing these antelope was going to tax the team, as not only were they considerably bigger than the Impala, but also they liked to live in thicker bush, rather than out on the grassland of the plains. Their size made it easier for Polly, as they had bigger rumps. However their weight meant that her hypodermic darts would be filled to capacity. They would therefore be heavier. Unless they could get very near, Polly would have to allow for a fall in the dart's trajectory.

It took them two full days to capture the four waterbuck. The males had broad strongly ringed horns. Hak was constantly worried for Polly's safety. At least the two females did not have horns.

Polly always loved Wildebeest, as she thought they looked liked old men. She smiled to herself. She would tease Dick that he would soon look like a Wildebeest. She suspected that he would give her 'a bit of that', for being so cheeky. She was looking forward to that. She was a little sad, when Josiah told her that he had received a telephone message from the Veterinary Department to say that Dick was going to be delayed. Polly therefore decided to set off for

Masailand and delay capturing the species which they still required that were available locally, on the Athi Plains.

They set up camp in the same place, where she had cut herself. As she lay on her camp bed on the first night she remembered Dick's very naughty kiss. When she thought about it, the boldness had been very out of character. She was certain that Dick would never have 'got into her knickers' nearly so soon, if he hadn't kissed her. She touched the arrow and giggled. She had changed. Most of the time now, she could not wait for him. She wanted him so much that she held him and directed him. She made a metal note to let him take the lead more often. She knew any delay would be likely to heighten both their pleasures.

Polly noticed how much happier everyone was in camp, when they did not have to worry about a paying client. In many ways they had to work harder making the pens and lifting the animals. However they didn't have to worry about mess or wash tents. Polly was not too bothered, if the men saw her in the shower.

The blowpipe had arrived so Polly spent the time practicing, when they were not capturing the bigger plains game. The first species that they went after was the Topi. Polly still strapped herself to the mattress, but she used the dart gun. Topi are much more nervous and so she knew she would have a longer shot. However all went according to plan and they captured a male and a female.

They had problems with capturing the Klipspringer. They were lucky with the male. They came across one, when they had set out after a Bushbuck. Polly was on the mattress. She quickly had to load a dart with a smaller volume. She placed a good shot and the animal went down before it had climbed too high on a rocky outcrop. Then they spent the rest of the day tracking a female, mainly on foot. Polly was so pleased that they were successful that day. She did not like the thought of an animal being on its own in the camp without another member of its species next to it.

The first species she captured with the blowpipe was a Dikdik. They were plentiful around the camp, but they are the smallest antelope and only stand a foot high. Luckily Gideon could get the Landrover near to them so Polly could shoot out of the side of the vehicle with the window taken off. She thought that using the blowpipe lying down on the mattress would be difficult. In fact she was wrong. She laughed to herself, that she must have improved her bust after all. In fact she just had a pillow under her breasts. She also found that a pillow made it more comfortable when she was firing the crossbow. She wondered if having a pillow under her breasts and two pillows under her bottom would be comfortable for her making love. She could not wait for Dick to come home.

She was sad, when they returned from Masailand and there was no word from Dick. Initially she was not concerned, as his message had not said how long he would be delayed. Also she had a lot to do in the camp supervising all the animals. She loved it that they became tame so quickly. They started to risk putting the male and female together of the smaller species. They did not seem to fight and seemed to become tamer sooner. Slowly they did this for the larger species. This also seemed to work well. Polly decided that probably the smaller species could travel together. This, she thought would be less stressful for them.

As there was no word from Dick, Polly continued capturing the game she required on the Athi plains. She used the dart gun for the biggest antelope, the Eland. Both sexes have horns. They stand at six feet and can jump amazingly high for an animal which weighs over half a ton. Getting them into their crates in the lorry was a real mission. Polly wondered, however she would manage, if she needed to capture a rhino or a hippopotamus.

They had managed that day to dart two Coke's Hartebeest which all the local Kenyans call Kongoni. This is the Swahili name. Polly wondered why this was. Kenyans never called Wildebeest, Gnu which is their Swahili name.

She was having a cup of tea, when she got a call from Mobia. He sounded concerned. He had received no word from Dick who was now well over due. He had just spoken to the Veterinary Department HQ and they had heard nothing. Polly was very tempted to drive to the HQ in the morning, but realised it would be pointless and would just look, as if she was over nervous fiancé.

Chapter 10

Dick is definitely missing

Three mornings later, Mobia rang again he obviously now was seriously worried. He had heard from the Veterinary Department that the Government Landrover which Dick had been using had returned with Mbaruk and a veterinary scout. The message Mobia had received was that Dick had totally disappeared. All the rest of the veterinary staff were fine and were still in Tana River District searching for him. They had been hampered by the very heavy rain both locally and upcountry. Mobia did not know anymore. Polly did not hesitate. She told Mobia that she would go to the HQ and then call on him, when she knew more.

Polly had never met the Director of Veterinary Services (DVS). The DVS was a mature Kikuyu who had qualified as a veterinary surgeon at Edinburgh Vet School. He didn't suffer fools gladly. Nor did he like being talked down to by Europeans. Polly knew that Dick liked the DVS and thought he was a good leader. She did not know that the DVS respected Dick. However Polly was well aware that she needed any help that the DVS could offer her to find Dick.

The DVS had the door of his office open. He wondered who this young Kikuyu girl was who was joking with the old man who was in charge of the registry which contained all the veterinary files. It was an unusual thing for a young girl to say to an old man that he had better look lively, if he wanted to purchase her as a bride, as she was already spoken for. The DVS pulled the door open, as Polly was in the act of knocking. She smiled at him, saying in Kikuyu,

"I'm sorry to bother you Sir. I'm afraid I have not got an appointment to see you." He answered her rather rudely in Kikuyu,

"Who are you?" Still smiling, Polly answered,

"I know I'm a little young, but I'm Richard Brendon's fiancé. I gather he is missing making a path for a new stock route in Tana River District. I am rather concerned and I wondered if you could give me a little more information, before I leave to go up there to

85

look for him." Polly offered him her hand. Because he was so surprised he shook it in the two handed African way. He was even more surprised by her strong grip, as she responded with two hands. At that moment the European Deputy Director came in. The DVS was so shaken that he continued to speak in Kikuyu,

"I don't think it is very advisable for you to go and look for him. The area is very large and very wild." Polly answered in a very friendly manner,

"It is kind of you to be concerned for my safety, but I have spent my whole life in wild areas, my father was Hector Cavendish." The DVS nodded in recognition. His Deputy obviously did not understand Kikuyu, but he had met Polly's father. He butted in,

"You must be Polly. Dick has spoken of you. He is a very lucky man. You are an extremely beautiful young girl." Polly laughed and continued in English,

"Thank you for the compliment. The inclusion of the word young has not gone unnoticed. I'm probably actually younger than I look, but I run a very efficient hunting team. Gideon the hunter and I are very familiar with the NFD. I was surprised that Dick did not bother to take a Long Wave Band (LWB) radio." The DVS, who was exceptionally intelligent, now had recovered himself. He replied in English.

"I can't think why he didn't. I know they need a high aerial. I imagine there are not any tall enough trees. They also had two vehicles. The whole scenario is very strange. Dick disappeared at night without trace. I can't believe he was taken by a wild animal. There surely would have been some evidence. I know all his team are devoted to him, so I'm confident that there was no foul play."

Polly's heart sank. This was very much more serious than she had imagined.

"Well if you could furnish me with a letter to his staff to introduce me. I would be very grateful. I have already met the DC and the Chief of Police at Galole. However I gather from the weather reports that I would need to go in from the southern end of the projected stock route, as the northern area is flooded. The veterinary staff did well to get out. It would also be very helpful, if I could have a word with Mbaruk and the veterinary scout who raised the alarm."

The DVS turned to the DDVS and said.

86

"Can you get them send for, Gerald? If you could ask my secretary to come in and I will dictate a letter. May I call you Polly? Would you like a cup of tea?"

"I would be delighted if you call me Polly and I would love a cup of tea. I have been meaning to invite you to my home, as I wanted your advice. I did not want embarrass Dick, but I have had a change of career and I'm now trapping game animals rather than killing them."

They were alone again and the DVS smiled at her,

"It is sad that we are all so worried about Dick, but today is a first for me. A European girl comes in to my office and until I see her I think she is a Kikuyu. Then she invites me to her home. Kenya is changing very rapidly." Polly added,

"Hopefully it is changing for the better."

The discussion with Mbaruk and the veterinary scout was carried out in Swahili. Polly did not learn much more, but she was delighted that the DVS instructed Mbaruk and the veterinary scout to take the Landrover back the way they had come to Tana River District, to lead Polly and her crew back to the rest of the veterinary team. Apparently they had got out of the area by coming through Tsavo East Game Park and crossing the Galana River at a ford south of Luggard's falls. They reported that Polly's lorry and Landrover would have no difficulties. They said that the water level in the Galana was falling and the surface water was diminishing.

Polly took everyone she could possibly spare from the ranch. It was far from ideal, as there were a large number of new animals. However she put them all on a bonus, as it would not be fair only to give bonuses to the men who came with her, as she knew those which had been left behind would have to work harder. She already paid some of the older sons and daughters of the staff to help with the new animals, when they got home from school. She had noticed that the teenage girls who would, in years gone by, have been wives at that age were particularly caring with the game animals. She, like the DVS had observed, was aware that things were happening in this old colony very fast.

On the journey up north she prayed that they were on a fool's errand and that she would find Dick safe and sound, when she arrived at their camp. Her hopes were immediately dashed. There

87

was no Dick. They had absolutely no new news and there was an air of despondency in the camp. Miraculously, perhaps because of her linguistic skills, or because of the letter from the DVS, the moral instantly improved after she gave them all a short address to introduce her and her staff. In fact she made them all laugh by telling a very crude joke. She told them that she was so impressed with how Dick had made the bulls mate at the CAIS that she had let him mate her which was why she had a ring on her finger. She said that it was up to them all to find Dick, or there would be no wedding, or more importantly no party. She thought that the veterinary staff were probably surprised that she had travelled up with the men in her lorry. She had left her Landrover at home in case there was an emergency and they needed transport to go into Nairobi urgently.

Miss Clemenceau had been right in her assessment of Polly. She was a very competent, caring leader. Everyone who worked with her soon respected her for her hard work and her attention to detailed planning. While her team was settling into the camp she asked each of the men from the Veterinary Department to have a chat with her so that she could try to figure out how Dick had completely disappeared. It certainly helped, as she could speak in their tribal languages. She learnt how two members of the staff had been surprised, when they were having a walk after the heavy rain to have walked into a hippo which had mercifully run away from them rather than charging them. She realised that this was probably why they thought that Dick had been taken by a wild animal. Polly soon realised that the Veterinary Staff might well be very good at dealing with cattle, but they were not familiar with game animals like her team.

Now she could see at first hand the effect of the heavy rain as well as the difficulties of travelling on a compass bearing. She was going to have to alter her approach, when looking for Dick. Her questioning brought out several helpful pieces of information. One of the men was certain that there was a panga missing. This meant that Dick had taken it with him to blaze the trees, so he could follow his way back to the camp. However they could find no evidence of any marks on the trees near to the camp. Also Polly noted that he had not taken his shot gun, so he had not gone bird shooting. Polly then tried to find out if he had taken a torch or a water bottle. She knew if

88

Mobia had been with him in the camp that Mobia would have known the answers, but she was well aware that the veterinary staff had many other jobs and looking after Dick had not been one of them. All she could be certain was that he had left silently in the night taking a panga.

Then she got her big break with her enquires. She asked about food. She was told about Dick supplying the camp with bird meat. Then she was told how he had tried to vary the diet. They had even eaten big flying ants which Dick had covered in batter and then had deep-fat fried. Apparently they had been delicious. She was told that Dick had fried some of the big land snails in garlic. When she asked what they tasted like, she was told that they didn't really know, as no one else had tried them. Apparently Dick had said they were very rubbery. Polly asked,

"When had Dick eaten the snails?"

"He had eaten them for supper on the night he had disappeared."

"Were they certain?"

"Yes they were certain, because there was some laughter and Dick had said that he would not be eating them again, as he felt a little sick."

At last Polly knew some of the answers. Polly guessed that Dick had felt sick, when he went to bed after eating the snails. He had woken in the night and realised that he had to go to the loo. He had taken the panga to dig a hole. He had probably taken some loo roll and a box of matches, as that was what he normally did, so that he could burn the loo paper and cover his excrement with soil in the hole which he had dug with the panga. Polly knew that Dick was rarely really ill, but very often had diarrhoea.

Polly discussed her findings with Hak. They had already looked in Dick's tent. Any trace of Dick's footprints would have long since been obliterated. However they knew roughly in which direction he would have left the camp. Polly also thought that he had probably not gone very far, as it was night time and she thought he probably had been pretty desperate to go to the loo.

Hak found two burnt matches and fragments of burnt loo roll. It was only after a wider search that they found a torch and the panga. Polly thought that the most likely scenario was that Dick had walked the wrong way after going to the loo. He had collapsed and dropped the torch, which now had a spent battery, together with the panga. He had then got up again and walked out into the bush and got totally lost.

Polly despaired. She would not admit to herself that he was dead. Why was there no body? Polly, Gideon and Hak talked long into the night. Eventually they all went to their beds, after they had made a plan for the morning.

Polly was worried about the veterinary staff for two reasons; they had been away from their homes for a long time which they were not used to and they were not very familiar with bush craft in this type of terrain. She certainly did not want any of them getting lost which would compound the problem.

She got on to the Veterinary Department on the radio and had a message sent to the DVS to keep him fully in the picture. She got them to pack up their camp and proceed back to Kabete. They would take the route that she had come up on which Mbaruk was now very familiar with. Mbaruk would drive the Landrover and Pius would drive the lorry. She made sure that they had enough fuel, water and food.

She got Noah to bring the Landrover up to their camp with her pack donkey called Muffin which her father had bought for her when she was three years old. He had a well-made pack saddle. Gideon organised all their team to start searching in pairs for Dick. There still was no sign of vultures in the sky which was reassuring, but Polly was close to tears, as she knew Dick might have gone a considerable distance.

Chapter 11

Dick's life is in the balance

Dick recovers consciousness. He remembers having violent diarrhoea and collapsing in the night. It is still dark he can't find his torch or panga, but he thinks he knows the direction of the camp. He knows that it can't be very far away. He sets off walking. After about twenty minutes he realises that he is lost so he sensibly sits down with his back to a small tree and waits for the dawn so that he can get his bearings. He goes to sleep. He wakes with the sun rising in the East. He thought he had initially left the camp in a westerly direction so he walks east into the rising sun.

He feels unwell, but actually he does not feel too bad. He drinks from a puddle of surface water which he knows is far from ideal, but he thinks he must do everything to prevent dehydration. He was correct that he was to the west of the camp. Sadly in the night he had walked south, so that now he missed the camp which was to his left. He walked on to the east. He knew he was soon going to have to stop, as he would get lost again with the sun getting high in the sky. The bush was not that thick, but he had not got the height like he had in the back of the lorry and he could not see a tree to take a bearing on. All the trees were acacias with sharp thorns and he could not climb them. Luckily he had on his gym shoes, but he did not have a hat. His only piece of clothing was his kikoi.

He found some shade and nodded into a stupor. He was exhausted and totally lacking in energy, but at least he had water. He slept fitfully. His thoughts wandered to Polly. He knew she was busy game capturing. He hoped she had got his message. He was fairly certain that she would have done. He didn't want her to worry about him. However he knew he was in a potentially very dangerous situation. He had to keep his spirits up. He had to keep thinking rationally. He had to keep himself hydrated. He knew that the surface water was disappearing fast.

With great strength of will he made himself get up as the sun was setting. With it at his back, he managed to keep walking. He stopped and drank at every puddle. He managed to keep going until the rapid African dusk enveloped him. He stopped near a large puddle and drank greedily. He forced himself to keep drinking until he felt totally bloated. Then he sat once again with his back to a tree. Soon he could see the wonderful canopy of the stars. He could make out the Southern Cross. He got up again and continued walking wearily east. It was difficult in the dark. However he was aware of a game trail which seemed to be heading east. He followed it until he was just too exhausted to continue. He sank down beside a puddle which he realised was very shallow. He managed to drink. He was still thinking rationally. He realised his source of water was disappearing fast.

When he woke with the sun, he knew he was in real trouble. The ground was dry. The puddle had gone. He thought that he probably only had three hours left to live. It was his desire to see Polly again and not to cause her any grief that spurred him into action. He staggered on into the sunrise. He followed a game trail. Eventually the sun was too high to guide him. He stuck with the game trail. He knew it was his only hope. He had seen no surface water that morning.

He collapsed on the path. His last thoughts were of Polly. He had let her down.

He was barely alive, when he was found the following morning by two Wakamba girls, Ruth aged eight and Sita aged six. They were herding their mother's goats. They and their mother, Gertrude had come to down from Kitu district two years ago. Their father had been killed by a lorry on the road. He had been a water carrier. Gertrude had been left with two little girls, a donkey and cart, together with a small herd of goats. A man had moved into the village and had taken over the water carrying business. Gertrude was a courageous woman and was determined to make a new life for herself and her small family. She came down off the Yatta Plateau during the rainy season and journeyed through the barren dry Tana River District. As now, the surface water had rapidly receded, when the rains ceased. She had brought plenty of water and so managed to journey on until she found, what appeared to be a permanent water hole. To her horror she found the reason why there were no local people living at the water hole. In the water was a very bad tempered hippo.

Somehow Gertrude and the two girls had managed to avoid being killed by the hippo. They made sure that they never became between the animal and the water in the early morning. Equally they were very careful not to be anywhere near the animal when it came looking for forage at dusk. They had lived a precarious existence, particularly the previous year, as the rains had failed. The water in the water hole became much diminished, but they had survived with their goats and the donkey.

This year the recent rains had been a life saver. The hippo had disappeared. Gertrude thought it had returned to the Tana River which was probably fifty miles to the east. The water hole was full. Gertrude had planted some maize hoping the rains would come. The plants were now flourishing.

The two girls thought Dick was dead. Ruth stayed with the body and the goats. Sita ran to her mother. Gertrude initially, also thought Dick was dead. However she put her cheek near to his mouth and felt a small movement of air. She left both girls with him and the goats and returned to the water hole. It took her sometime to locate all the harness for the donkey, but eventually she brought the donkey and cart the three miles to Dick. Although she was a strong woman, it was extremely difficult for her and the girls to load Dick on to the cart. Gertrude was alarmed by the bright red colour of Dick's exposed skin. All the time she kept trickling water from a gourd into his mouth. Only occasionally did she see him swallow. However she persisted. Eventually they all returned to the water hole. They dragged Dick into the small hut. He seemed to be burning, although it was well past the heat of the day and the air temperature was not hot for the area. She had laid him on a mat. She covered him with his kikoi which she kept soaking wet. All the time she tried to get him to drink little volumes of water.

She had more success with warm goat's milk. All through the night and the following day she kept up the milk. Dick continued to burn. Gertrude was so grateful that she had plenty of water at hand. A month earlier she and the girls had to be very frugal with water. The heavy rains had saved them.

It was only, as she was giving him some water at evening time, that she realised he had passed some urine. She then had a little hope that this large European would survive. However she wondered how he had arrived, where the girls had found him, with no water, or food and only a single piece of cloth. He surely must have been over a hundred miles from either the Sabaki or the Tana River. It was extremely rough country and she knew of few Africans who journeyed through. Certainly she had never seen a European.

It was two more days, before Dick regained consciousness. He had blisters from the sun on large areas of his skin. However the pain had diminished. He was disorientated and totally confused. All he could remember was trying to walk to the east. Gertrude's face materialised before his eyes. He managed to croak in Swahili,

"Thank you." Then he drank greedily from the gourd of water, before flopping back down on to the sleeping mat.

Gertrude and the girls carried on with their normal tasks for the day. The girls did not find this strange white man unpleasant, but they could not understand why his skin looked so funny. They had never seen a European before. Gertrude had little experience with Europeans, but told the girls how lucky they were to have brown skin which was not damaged by the sun.

Gertrude realised that food was going to be a problem for them all. The lactating goats were their saviours and they had plenty of milk. The rains, which had made the grass and the bushes so green, had increased their milk supply overnight. However she knew it would be some weeks before the new maize would be edible. She was grateful for the disappearance of the hippo, but she still had to maintain the thorn fences to keep off other animals from the attractive maize plants. Only once in her life had she seen a herd of elephants. She remembered what havoc they had caused.

She knew the man was very thin. She had nobly tried him with a little of the precious maize meal. He had choked and, so she was happy to give him the plentiful goat's milk. She was slightly concerned that he had not passed any faeces. Common sense told her that he had not eaten any solid food for days and therefore did not have anything to pass. He now regularly urinated. This caused him acute embarrassment. The last time he had tried to get up, but he was just too weak.

That night she had woken. He was trying to stand. She guessed that he wanted to urinate. She helped him to stand. Leaning heavily on her he had managed to get outside of the hut. He said in Swahili,

"Thank you for your help. I am so sorry to defile your home. You have been so kind to me." Without thinking she replied in Wakamba her native language,

"Do not worry." She was very surprised, when he very hesitantly replied in her language,

"Thank you." She had never heard a European speak in her language. It was very strange. She remembered, when she was very young that a white baby had been born in the village. The baby had died and her parents had said that was probably a good thing as white Wakamba babies were not normal.

She replied in Wakamba, but immediately realised that he did not understand, so she reverted to Swahili. He then said in Swahili,

"I am sorry I do not speak Wakamba, but my wife to be, speaks it fluently." This statement confused Gertrude. What did he mean? Surely a man of his age had at least one wife. He was a very big man. Gertrude was surprised that he did not have three wives.

Gertrude realised how weak he was, as he was leaning more on to her. She helped him back into the hut and on to the sleeping mat. She gave him some more goats' milk and also some water. Then he slept.

Gertrude was concerned as he did not wake at dawn. The two girls made a considerable amount of noise, as did the goats and the donkey. However he was in a very deep sleep. She set about her chores, but kept checking him, as it did not seem to be right that he was in such a deep sleep.

In fact Dick was totally exhausted. He felt much better towards evening time. He tried to get up on his own, but he could not manage it. Gertrude heard him and helped him. He apologised for all the problems that he was causing. Gertrude did her best to reassure him. She was so relieved that he seemed a little better. She had worried that he was going to die. Then she would not have known what to do. She worried that if she just buried him, then someone might come looking for him and think that she had killed him.

Dick was now trying to remember what had happened. He now could recall having violent diarrhoea and vomiting. He could also remember thinking how stupid he had been eating the snails. Then

95

there was a complete gap in his memory until he was struggling to walk in the hot sun in an easterly direction. Then he had woken up with this Wakamba lady and her two children. There did not seem to be any other people which he thought was odd. With her help he had managed to have a wee a few yards from the hut. Now he managed to sit on a big log with his back to the wall of the hut. He had managed to drape his kikoi over him, to hide his modesty. He realised that the lady was not worried that he was virtually naked. Her two girls were naked, but she was wrapped in a bright kikoi. He indicated to her to join him on the log. She sat down and Dick asked,

"Are these two girls your children?" Gertrude nodded her head.

"What are their names? I am called Dick." She repeated,

"Dick." Then she said,

"They are called, Ruth and Sita. I am called Gertrude." Dick asked,

"Are there other villagers?"

"No there are only us. My husband was killed by a lorry. Nobody wanted us, so we left Kitui District to try and find a better life."

Dick was amazed that this brave woman was all alone. He now felt doubly guilty, as he had been drinking all her valuable goats' milk and caused her all this extra work. He rightfully realised that the veterinary team had not known what had happened to him, or they would have found him. He did not know what to do. He knew he did not have enough strength to walk anywhere. He thought it was not right for him to commandeer the donkey and cart. She must have read his thoughts as she said very emphatically,

"You will stay here with us until you are much stronger. We will look after you. We will manage somehow. We have a little food." Dick replied,

"Thank you. You are very kind." He felt that was totally inadequate. He was saved from further conversation by the arrival of the girls and the goats.

He continued to sit on the log, although he felt a little dizzy. Soon Ruth brought him a gourd of warm milk for him to drink. He said, in Swahili,

"Thank you. You are very kind." She obviously did not understand. Gertrude called out something in Wakamba. Ruth smiled at him. When Gertrude brought him her gourd, he asked her in Swahili,

"What is thank you. You are very kind, in Wakamba?" Gertrude told him. He memorised it and then repeated it. Ruth smiled at him.

The following day Dick felt much stronger. He managed to get out of the hut on his own. Gertrude came with him as she was obviously worried that he would fall. After he had a wee he sat on the log and Ruth brought him her gourd. He said in Wakamba,

"Thank you. You are very kind." He received a smile and a giggle. From then on he tried to learn Wakamba. He soon realised that like Gertrude the girls were very intelligent.

Chapter 12

Polly and Hak set out to find Dick

The capture team hunted for any trace of Dick for two days without any luck. They were hampered because the heavy rain made tracking impossible. What they needed to find were tracks made after the heavy rain had stopped. On the third day, while the team searched an even wider area, Polly and Hak set out with the donkey to carry water and a little food in a direct line from the camp in an easterly direction as Hak rightly thought that would have been Dick's most likely route. They got lucky. So marking the spot with a large number of tree blazes, they returned to camp to report to Gideon who was coordinating everything.

Gideon and Polly agreed that now that they had a track to follow and the weather looked settled, it was best for all of them except for Polly and Hak to return to the ranch. Polly assured Gideon that she would be totally safe with Hak and leaving Noah with a Landrover in camp was not sensible. Noah looked relieved. He did not want to be left alone in the middle of Tana River District.

Polly and Hak with the donkey managed to get back to the same spot which they had reached earlier in the day. Hak thought they could risk both of them sleeping, as he had not seen any evidence of lion. Polly was well aware that lion are very liable to kill donkeys. They made Muffin a small thorn boma. Poly slept with her shot gun beside her and Hak had his spear. The night was uneventful and they were glad that they both had had a good nights slept and were ready for a very long trek, as soon as it was light enough for Hak to see Dicks' tracks.

It was sandy soil and they made good progress. Hak led. Polly followed him leading the donkey. They hardily stopped until Hak called a halt in the quick falling dusk. They made a donkey boma and gave Muffin some hay and short feed. Polly was surprised how little water he drank. She was extremely thirsty. Hak let her drink her fill. He said it was so much more sensible to drink at night. Drinking in the heat of the day just made one sweat more. Polly did not sleep well. She had not needed Hak to tell her that Dicks' steps were becoming shorter. She was so worried about him. She had visions of arriving too late. There was absolutely no surface water now.

They were swiftly away in the morning. Dick's tracks indicated that he was staggering now. Then to Polly's amazement they heard a donkey braying. They thought they were coming to a village. Muffin brayed in return. Hak said he could smell a waterhole. They increased their pace. They met the two girls and the goats. Ruth asked in Wakamba, if they had come for the European. Polly replied in the same language and asked if he was well. She was not surprised to hear that he was sick. The girls and the goats ran ahead of them to the hut. Polly had tears in her eyes, as she saw Dick stagger to his feet. She ran to him,

"Oh Dick, I have been so worried about you. You were such a fool to eat those snails." Dick held her in his arms. Polly could feel how weak he was. She immediately helped him to sit on the log. She turned to Gertrude, as Hak put his hand on Dick's shoulder. Polly said in Wakamba,

"What is your name? You have saved his life." Then Polly hugged Gertrude, who laughed,

"Thank goodness you speak good Wakamba. Dick's Wakamba is very bad."

Polly introduced Hak who to her surprise also spoke Wakamba. Her mind was in a whirl, but she tried to concentrate on the essentials. She made Dick take four 'Nivaquin' tablets which were a curative dose for Malaria. She knew he could not have been taking any prophylaxis. Dick gagged. Polly commanded,

"Don't be sick. Breathe through your nose." Gertrude interrupted,

"Goats' milk is the only nourishment he has had. He chokes on maize meal." Polly's rejoinder was,

"We will have to alter that or he will blow away. He is so thin." Gertrude smiled,

"I think I want to be a European. You are so fierce with men. Dick tells me that you are not actually his wife yet, but only betrothed to him. I thought a big man like him would have at least three wives." It was Polly's turn to laugh,

"I'm glad his Wakamba is so bad. He can't understand us. I have no intention of letting him have another wife. I do love him with all my heart, but I have to keep him in order!"

No more was said, but it was obvious to them all, including Dick that he was too weak to go anywhere in his present state. The girls took the goats out to browse. Hack fed the two donkeys after he had unloaded Muffin. He gave all the food which they had brought to a very grateful Gertrude. Polly just sat next to Dick and held his hand.

Gertrude thought it was miraculous how Dick's health improved so rapidly after Polly's arrival. It might have been the anti-malarial tablets, but her very presence seemed to lift his spirits. Every time he looked at her he smiled. It made Gertrude think that it would perhaps be nice to have a husband again.

There had been no discussion, but Gertrude just asked Polly if she and her daughters could come with them. Polly was pleased, as she knew that Dick owed his life to Gertrude and she also knew she would do anything to help her. Apart from that she liked her. Also she was picking up vibes that Hak also liked her. The two girls were a delight to them all.

The following day Hak carried out a reconnaissance. He was away two and a half days, but he managed to reach the Tana River. He thought they probably would be able to make the journey in four days.

Two days later they set off. Gertrude's donkey pulled the cart which carried Dick who was still not able to walk more than a hundred yards without resting. It also carried all Gertrude's possessions, the food and some water. Polly's donkey carried more water and the donkey fodder. Hak led the way with the girls herding the goats. Polly and Gertrude led the donkeys. On the second day they were lighter as they had less water. Dick was stronger and insisted that he could walk. They covered much further, so they reached the Tana River on the evening of the third day. Just before they reached the river they crossed the Garissa to Garsen Road.

They took this road on the following day. There was not much traffic, about one vehicle an hour. In the late morning a Game Department Landrover stopped. The District Game Department Officer knew Dick and he had heard that he was missing. He was very relieved that he had survived. He wanted to take Dick to

100

Garsen, but Dick said there was no way he was going to leave the others. However the District Game Department Officer said he would get the Senior Veterinary Scout at Garsen to contact the Veterinary Department HQ at Kabete and pass on the good news. Polly also asked him to give a message to Gideon so that he could meet them at Garsen.

The travelling took on a festive air. Polly and Dick were often holding hands. Polly noticed Hak and Gertrude spend time together. The girls enjoyed walking with Dick and Polly. They started to learn Swahili and Dick tried to improve his Wakamba. The lorry was waiting for them at Garsen in the veterinary compound. Gideon and Noah were delighted to see them.

As there was several hours of daylight left they decided to journey to the Veterinary Holding Ground at Sabaki. This was only five miles North of Malindi.

The best route back to the ranch on the Athi Plains was via Mombasa and then up the main Mombasa to Nairobi Road. The following morning they crossed the big metal bridge across the Sabaki River and went through the new tourist destination of Malindi. It was an easy forty mile journey then, to the ferry across Kilifi creek. Ruth and Sita were fascinated by the sea out on their left. Polly was delighted as Dick bought some cashew nuts for them all. She did not realise that Dick loved them. It was the first solid food he had eaten. They had a further forty miles to Mombasa which involved crossing Mtwapa creek. There was a good bridge, but they charged a toll. Gideon elected to cross on the old hand pulled ferry. This was exciting for Ruth and Sita as the men sang, as they pulled. It was called the 'singing ferry'.

They crossed on to Mombasa Island on the Nyali Bridge and then left the Town of Mombasa via a causeway. On the left at the far end of the causeway was the Mombasa Veterinary Department. They arrived just before 4.00 pm. The staff were just about to go home. Polly was pleased to see Dick was very popular. The office messenger brought them all some beautiful pawpaw which he grew in his garden. The Veterinary Officer, called Mike offered for Dick and Polly to come to stay with him. However Dick thanked him and said they would stay with the rest.

Polly was worried about Dick, as he just collapsed on his camp bed. He assured her he was not ill, but totally exhausted. She made him eat some pawpaw. Gideon and Hak crossed the road to a butcher's shop which was by the gate of the Kenya Meat Commission Abattoir. They bought some beef which they roasted. Polly thought was delicious. She was sad that Dick would not eat any. However she made him eat some rice and some bananas. It was a happy camp.

They were all up early in the morning to finish the final two hundred and eighty miles to the ranch. Hak had a long conversation with Polly. Gertrude and her two girls were going to move in with him. He knew they had too many goats, so he said he would make arrangements for the majority to be sold which would help Gertrude to buy clothes for the girls, particularly school uniforms. He said Gertrude was very grateful as Dick had said that he was going to pay their school fees.

The hunting staff gave Dick a big welcome, when they eventually arrived. Polly saw that Dick did his very best to greet them all. She could see that he was about to collapse, so she soon had him sitting comfortably on her veranda. She got Josiah to make a very light supper. She ate with him to make sure he ate a decent amount. They both had showers and were soon in bed. Polly lay on top of him. She kissed his neck and then burst into tears. Dick stroked her hair. She sobbed,

"I thought you had died. I did not know how I would live without you. Oh it is so lovely to have you here in my bed. Now you must sleep."

Chapter 13

The DVS comes to lunch

Josiah brought through Polly's tea. Dick was still fast asleep so she wriggled out of bed without waking him. She went out to check on all the animals before breakfast. She was delighted that they all had settled in so well. She had a chat with Gideon, as now they were slightly behind schedule with their catching. She was glad that all the species that she still needed could be caught near the ranch on the Athi plains. She made arrangements for them to start in the morning. Gideon had already telephoned the rancher, where they intended to operate.

She sat down to breakfast and started opening her post. To her delight there was a letter from a wildlife park in Texas which wanted a whole consignment of plains game. Luckily she read the whole letter carefully. The American veterinary authorities required that all the animals were quarantined on an island which had no resident cloven-hoofed animals. They were to be blood tested for Foot and Mouth Disease (FMD) on arrival on the island and again three weeks later. If they were healthy and passed both tests they could then be shipped to the USA.

The only islands that Polly knew of in Kenya were up North near Lamu. She knew that they all had a resident population of cattle, because Dick had told her the difficulties that he had had of providing them with an AI service. She had a brainwave. When it was 8.30 am and Kabete HQ had opened she was going to ring the DVS and thank him for his help in finding Dick. She was also going to tell him how weak Dick was and that she thought he should have at least a week off work. She knew Dick would object, but she was sure the DVS would agree. She decided she would invite the DVS for lunch. He could then see how weak Dick was, for himself. Also she could ask the DVS about this American quarantine requirement.

As soon as she gave her name to the PA to the DVS, she was put straight through to him. In his abrupt way he immediately asked after

Dick. There was obviously no time for pleasantries on his agenda. Polly told him that she had got Dick home last night and that he was still very weak. She did not hesitate and immediately asked him for lunch, so that he could assess Dick for himself. He was delighted with this unexpected invitation and so he said he would be pleased to accept. He said he would look forward to seeing her at lunchtime. Before he could ring off Polly thanked him for his prompt help in finding Dick. She said she was extremely grateful, but would not mention it again as she guessed that Dick and he would be embarrassed. Polly was pleased as he ended the conversation by saying that she was a very wise young lady.

Polly then went to warn Josiah that there would be four of them for lunch, as she was going to ask Gideon, so that he could have an input about the animal quarantine arrangements. She also told Josiah how Dick had a real problem with solid food, so could he make something suitable. She made Josiah laugh as she said,

"I have tried to get him to eat, but he won't listen to me. Hopefully he will listen to a wise old man, like you Josiah."

She was outside inspecting the animal pens, when Dick came out. She ran to him and put her arms around him. She hugged him to her,

"Did you enjoy your breakfast?"

"Josiah did his best, but I could only manage a banana." Polly decided on a different approach, as she led him back to the house. She smiled up at him,

"You know what I have been missing? I have been missing a 'bit of that'." She made a rude gesture with her forearm and added, "I want the big strong Dick back again. You will never get your strength back with just a banana for breakfast."

They sat at the table on the veranda. Josiah winked at Polly and brought out fresh toast, with coffee. There was butter, honey, marmalade and 'Marmite'. Polly cut the toast into slices and after preparing them, started to feed him. Initially he did not notice, but Polly managed to undo two more buttons of her shirt. She had not bothered to put on a bra, when she had got up. As she leant forward to feed him, she noticed him look down. He looked up into her sparkling mischievous eyes.

"This young heifer wants to be noticed."

104

"Polly you are marvellous. I love you with all my heart. Thank you for finding me. You have the most beautiful breasts. The sight of them is a great incentive to get strong. Please keep feeding me."

She told him she had invited the DVS and Gideon for lunch. She was surprised, as he seemed pleased. He was even more pleased, when he realised he would have a role to play in the animal export. He knew he was really good at finding the jugular veins in domestic animals. He was sure he would be able to adapt to taking blood from game animals. She made him come into her bedroom. He had a big grin on his face when she took off her shirt and put on a bra, saying,

"I had better behave myself with your boss coming to lunch, but there is no harm in you seeing what he is missing. Come on let me show you all the animals that we have caught. Some of them are becoming really tame."

Dick had gone to the lavatory, when the DVS drove up. Polly ran down the steps off the veranda to greet him. He seemed genuinely please to see her. She said,

"I have a confession. I have been a very wicked scheming girl, inviting you to lunch. I need your advice." He smiled,

"I am happy to give you advice. I also want to thank you for finding Dick. He is one of my best veterinary officers. I won't say that to his face, as I don't want him to become big headed." They walked up to the house, as Dick came out on to the veranda. Polly could sense how shocked the DVS was with Dick's appearance. They very formally shook hands. The DVS said with a smile,

"You had us all worried by your disappearance. I don't want such an escapade to be repeated!"

Gideon came to the house with the letter from America in his hand which Polly had given him earlier. Polly introduced him to the DVS as a professional hunter, but she also added that although Gideon was not happy with the role, he had very much taken over the role of her father. This made the DVS smile.

As they sat on the veranda for glasses of Josiah's homemade lemonade and lime, Gideon passed the letter to the DVS for him to read. The DVS took his time and read the letter twice. The others just sipped their lemonade and lime. When he had finished Polly said,

"I have been racking my brains to think of suitable islands; those up north have resident cattle together with sheep and goats, the islands in Lake Victoria would be totally unsuitable from a transport point of view and the islands on the Kenyan South Coast do not have any permanent water."

The DVS smiled an enigmatic smile,

"Have you considered Mombasa Island? There are cloven hoofed animals in Mombasa District, but they are not permitted on the Island."

Polly jumped to her feet.

"Sir you are a star. Thank you. I know Gideon and I will have many difficulties, but we will do our best to put your brilliant idea into practice. Let's have something to eat."

On cue Josiah brought in the food. It was a very happy meal. Polly could see that Dick was making a massive effort to follow the conversation, but she could see that exhaustion and lack of appetite was wearing him down. The DVS noticed and soon said that he needed to return to Kabete. Polly came with him to his car. When he was out of earshot he said.

"I know you will nurse him, but he needs a long period of rest. I will make sure the DDVS rises to the occasion and makes sure all Dick's duties are covered. However I will keep his interest up by organising a flight over the new stock route. That should not tax him too much. Also you could take him on the train down to Mombasa to set up a meeting about a quarantine station. You could stay at a beach hotel and get him really to relax."

Polly reached forward and kissed him on the cheek, saying,

"Thank you so much. I will take you up on your suggestions."

He waved out of the car window as he drove away.

Chapter 14

Polly makes the most of Dick's sick leave.

That night, Polly made sure that they went to bed early. She lay on top of him as normal and whispered to him,
"I don't want any 'humpy rumpy' as you are much too weak."
She reached down to him and giggled,
"It is lovely for me to feel you getting aroused. Sleep well, my darling."
Dick slept really well that night. He woke as Polly wriggled out of bed. He grabbed her thigh and pulled her back into bed, saying,
"Let's have five more minutes."
Josiah wisely delayed their morning tea for twenty minutes.
Polly knew Dick wanted to come to capture game on the following morning. After kissing him very passionately, when she woke up, she made him promise, if he did come that he would sit on the veranda of the ranch house, where they would be capturing the game. She said she would be very jealous, as the rancher had a pretty much younger wife who Polly new would fuss over him. She ended up by saying,
"If she unbuttons the top buttons of her shirt and I catch you taking a peek, I will kill you, however ill you are!"
Polly and the catching team worked hard. They kept going through lunch. It was only when Polly drew the operation to a halt at 5.00 pm that she had time to come up to the ranch house to find Dick. He was sitting having a cup of tea with the young wife and eating a large piece of cake. Polly in fact was pleased.
When they got into bed that night, Polly sat in the nude very provocatively on his tummy and asked,
"Were her breasts prettier than mine?"
"Oh no," replied Dick.

"Wrong think to say. That means that you did have a peep. I don't think I will allow you to suck mine as a punishment."

Dick pulled her body to him and sucked gently. Polly laughed,

"That is a vast improvement. I think Mr. Brendon you are on the mend."

To Polly's delight and Dick relief they then gently made love.

The capturing continued. Two days later Dick drove himself to Wilson Airport. He joined the water engineer and the senior veterinary scout who had been on the stock route making the original safari. Dick made notes of all that the elderly engineer said. He was relieved that they could see all the big white letters on the ground. They were not that clear, as the heavy rain had not been helpful. However they were clear enough to plan, where to put bore holes, and where to make dams.

Dick was pleased as there was only a gap of approximately fifty miles where there were no letters after he had gone missing. It was not difficult for the engineer to give his opinion on the sighting of two dams and one bore hole to fill in this gap in the stock route. They landed at Galana ranch which was on the north side of the Sabaki River, for lunch. Dick was relieved that they had started to make a causeway across the river. When that had been completed it would be an easy job for the Veterinary Department to walk the cattle across and then walk them down the Eastern border of Tsavo East National Park to Mackinnon Road. Mackinnon Road was on the Mombasa to Nairobi Railway and on the main Road. The Livestock Marketing Division (LMD) planned to have auctions there so that ranchers could easily move the cattle which they had purchased to their ranches.

As the DVS had advised, Polly booked them on the overnight train from Nairobi to Mombasa. She took Dick to his home so that he could tell Mobia what was happening. Polly had a shopping excursion into Nairobi to buy a new bikini, some sexy underwear and some sexy pyjamas. She liked sleeping in the nude, but she thought it would be fun to get Dick excited on the train. They got a Kabete driver to take them to the station.

Polly had never been on the train before and was looking forward to the journey. She dragged Dick along to speak to the driver after they had dropped their bags in their first class compartment. The driver was a friendly Sikh who had been a driver on this service for seventeen years. His stoker was a Wakamba. Polly joked with him in Wakamba. She said she knew he was really a European in disguise. He was just covered in coal dust. The stoker had a joke in return. He said he knew she was really a Wakamba girl as her Wakamba was so good. She was covered in white wash, as a disguise. Dick knew that Polly had, as usual, made a friend for life. He envied her easy manner with Africans.

They got on to the train and went immediately to the dining car. This was so Victorian that Polly was sure Prince Albert would come in at any moment. Dick told her that the food was excellent. They sat at a romantic table for two with a small light which glowed like a candle. There was also a single red rose in a small silver vase. Polly whispered to Dick that with the rose and the tiny light he was certainly going to 'get lucky' tonight. She had noticed that since his ordeal he had not had any alcohol. However he had a glass of sherry. She joined him, telling him she knew it was whisky which was meant to make girls frisky, but she could assure him that sherry had the same effect on her.

When she had tasted her soup, she whispered that she was sure the soup was laced with sherry. She enquired whether he would be 'up to it' tonight, as she was likely to be very frisky. She loved the feel of his hand under the table on her bare thigh. She assumed that meant he thought he was 'up to it'.

Dick had been right. The food was excellent. They had a small tilapia filet lightly grilled before their steaks. Polly licked her chocolate mousse round her lips in a very lascivious manner, as she knew he was watching her. The meal ended with an excellent cup of Kenyan coffee.

It was dark by the time they made their way down the corridor to their compartment. The seat had been altered so that there was now a top bunk. There were crisp white sheets. Polly was first to go to the loo. When she got back, she found that the compartment was empty. She guessed that Dick had gone to the loo at the other end of the carriage. When he arrived she was in her underwear. He held her from behind and gently kissed the back of her neck. She arched her back and reached behind it to undo her bra. As she hoped he covered her breasts with his hands. She turned in his arms and they kissed.

She then helped him out of his clothes. She could not be bothered to find her sexy pyjamas in her bag. She knew there was a ladder to help her up on to the top bunk, but she just put a foot on the lower bunk and gave a little spring so her body was half on to the top bunk. She felt his hands on her thighs, but he did not help her to get on to the upper bunk. He gently pulled down her knickers and buried his face between her thighs. It was lovely.

Eventually she got him on his back on the top bunk. They made love to the rhythm of the train. Polly was blissfully happy. She had her man, well and truly, back again.

They both slept very well and enjoyed the excellent breakfast which included porridge and kippers. Polly was so pleased that Dick had his appetite back for food and sex! They were met at the station by the Provincial Veterinary Officer (PVO) who took them to Nyali Beach Hotel. He was a jovial old vet who was enchanted by Polly. He had been friendly with Dick for many years. He teased him about being a confirmed bachelor and for being a 'cradle snatcher'. Dick was no longer concerned about his and Polly's big age gap. He took all the jokes in good spirits.

The PVO came into the hotel and after Dick had told him about his disastrous safari, they discussed the setting up of a game quarantine station. He had a possible site already in his mind. Apparently, recently, they had had a visit from 'The Great Indian Circus'. This had stayed for five weeks on a large open piece of ground with several large mango trees owned by the Town Council. The PVO was sure that the Council would rent it out to them.

After they had finished their coffee, and Dick and Polly had checked into the hotel, the PVO drove them back on to Mombasa Island to look at the site. It was ideal. There was a water supply and the circus had obviously been hooked up to the mains electricity in some way, as there was a pole with some taped up wiring. They then went to the Municipal offices. The clerk of the council was not about, as it was nearly lunch time, so they made an appointment for the following morning at ten o'clock. The PVO said he would pick them up.

The PVO dropped them back at the Nyali Beach Hotel. They had an enjoyable swim in the hotel pool. Dick was very complimentary about the new bikini. In the end they had a light lunch beside the pool. They then lay in the sun for a short time, before going back into the pool and just sitting in the water in the shallow end chatting. Polly asked what it was like for Dick, when he had run out of water in Tana River District. He tried to explain, what a nightmare it was. He said towards the end that he knew most of the time he was not being rational, but he just could not seem to think sensibly. Polly hugged him in the pool. She didn't need to say anything.

Towards the evening they had a lovely walk, hand in hand, along Nyali Beach. When it was getting dark the tide had come in and Polly dragged Dick into the sea. When they were in the water up to the middle of their chests, Polly wrapped her legs around his waist and her arms around his neck and then kissed passionately. Dick murmured,

"I think that I will get lost in Tana River District again." He was rewarded for that statement with,

"Don't you even joke about it?"

A very strong little hand went down the front of his swimming trunks and gripped him really quite hard to emphasise her point. Dick said,

"Your point is taken." She replied,

"Your point will only be taken tonight, if you promise to be careful in future. I never want to hear about you experimenting with eating, what the Australians call, 'Bush Tucker', again. No more snails are to be eaten!"

Dick smiled, as she lay in his arms that night. She might be fifteen years younger than him, but he knew she was a force to be reckoned with. He still never regretted asking her to marry him. He vowed never to be such a fool again, as he had been on the last safari. She stirred in his arms and they gently made love again.

After a great breakfast, they packed their bags so that they could vacant their room. They were already in the lobby when the PVO arrived. The PVO thought to himself, '*these two may be very much in love, but I appreciate their dedication to work.*'

The meeting at the municipal office was tedious, but Polly thought it had gone well. Obviously she had to go in alone, as she was going to be renting the land. Dick had gone with the PVO for a coffee. The official veterinary presence was not required. They had already agreed that the site would be acceptable to the Kenyan

Veterinary Department. Actually all Polly had to do was to agree on the rent and the terms of the lease. In fact they had a copy of the lease that the council had signed with the 'Great Indian Circus', so once the rent and the rental time had been agreed, everything was straight forward. It just seemed to take hours for the clerk to type up the document.

Polly wanted to make sure it was completed there and then, as she did not trust the post and did not want to have to make another trip down to Mombasa. This one had been great fun with Dick, but she knew that his presence had been sanctioned by the DVS. If she had to come back again just to sign the document, she would have to come on her own. When she eventually got out of the office, the messenger handed her a note from Dick.

My Darling Polly

The PVO has had to go to work at his office. I have gone to the Mombasa Club, also called 'The Chini Club' as it is down low on Tudor Creek. I will get us a room for the day. We can have lunch there and there is a nice pool. The Office Messenger says he will show you the way.

Lots of Love Dick

The Office Messenger was a Kikuyu and so soon he and Polly were in conversation. Polly persuaded him to take her a longer route through the 'Old Town'. This she found fascinating, as it had Arab architecture and was several hundreds of years old. The streets were narrow and dark. There were small Arab shops and Polly bought several small bags of different dried herbs and spices. There was a harbour and Polly went on board a dhow, so that an Arab trader could show her his carpets. She was very tempted to buy one.

Eventually she got to the 'Chini Club'. The Club Manager told her, their room number and pointed her in the correct direction. When she got to the room, she could hear an old fan clunking round. The door was unlocked. Dick was lying naked, on his back, asleep on the bed. She quietly locked the door. She started to undress, but notice his eyes briefly open. She was sure he was awake, but was pretending to be asleep. She undressed in a very sexy manner with her back to him. She bent down and rummaged into her bag. She found her new bikini.

Once she had put it on she turned to the bathroom and brought out a towel. She knew he was awake, as she could see his arousal. She had great difficulty in stopping herself from giggling. She wrapped the towel around her body and went towards the door. She wondered what he would do now that his bluff had been called.

"That was a very sexy little cameo. I really like the new bikini. Would you like to join me on the bed so that I can take it off again?"

She turned shedding her towel and smiled at him,

"Well Mr. Voyeur your body gave you away. I imagine you are up for a little pre-lunch activity."

She jumped on top of him and was astounded how he managed to pull the bows of her bikini so quickly. They were a little late for lunch. They spent a lovely afternoon by the pool, before taking a taxi to the railway station.

Polly sat on his knee in the carriage, as the train started its long uphill journey to Nairobi. It had to climb five and a half thousand feet and travel three hundred and ten miles. As the quick African darkness descended, they still had not reached the end of Dick's stock route at Mackinnon road which was fifty miles from Mombasa. They made their way to the restaurant car. They were too late to have a romantic table for two. They joined two young executives who were based in Mombasa and were travelling up to Nairobi on business. They were enchanted by Polly's arrival. Dick made some introductions. Roger was more outgoing. Chris was very shy.

It turned out that they both worked for an import/export company called 'Smith Mackenzie'. Over drinks and the meal, Polly found out exactly what they actually did for the company. She realised she would need their services, when she exported her game animals to Japan. She had already found out about moving them on the train to Mombasa, but they would have a role to play, organising the shipping and transport from the train to the docks. She immediately could tell that, although Roger appeared to have all the answers to her questions, it was Chris who was the bright one.

Roger told her that they lived in a large bachelor's mess down near the docks. He said she was welcome to stay, when she came down to Mombasa. Polly could tell he had designs for 'getting into knickers'. She was having none of that. She said very firmly,

"I always stay with my team. We camp with the animals." Roger made a big mistake,

"Surely it is not safe for a young European girl to camp with a group of Africans?" Polly frowned,

"I find that statement rather offensive. You have just asked me to stay in your bachelor's mess. I assume that I would have been quite safe there. I can assure you I am totally safe with my team, most of whom have known me since I was born." Roger coloured and only managed an unintelligible reply.

Polly was surprised as Chris said very sharply,

"Roger, I suggest you apologise immediately. I can assure you, Polly that such racial thinking is not the company policy nor does it fit with my personal sentiments." Roger murmured,

"I'm very sorry. I apologise unreservedly."

"Your apology is accepted and your statement has been forgiven, but not forgotten. I hope I can do business with your company and with both of you. Let's change the subject. Do you play rugby?"

Roger had lost his tongue, but Chris replied,

"Yes we both play for Mombasa Sports Club. In fact we have both played against you, Dick, twice. You thrashed us." He smiled at Polly,

"Perhaps it was not the ideal topic of conversation. Can I offer you both a brandy to go with your coffee?"

Dick and Polly both accepted. Roger to try and redeem himself, started talking about Brandy. He obviously knew about the subject. He was in charge of the liquor import side of the company in the whole of East Africa. Apparently one of their best sellers was locally bottled Gilbey's Gin. They brought it into Mombasa in big thirty five gallon plastic drums. They then bottled it in the industrial area in Nairobi. The company marketed it at seventeen Kenyan Shillings a bottle. Gordon's Gin which was their competitor was brought in already bottled and was marketed at eighteen Kenyan Shillings a bottle, so that they had the edge. Polly was not really interested in gin although she enjoyed drinking gin and tonic. However she casually asked,

"What happens to the thirty five gallon containers?"

"Oh we have got stacks of them at our depot in Nairobi."

"They would be very useful for watering my animals."

114

"You would be very welcome to them." He did not dare say that he would sell them to her. Polly did not miss a trick.

"That's really kind of you. I think we get in at 8.30 am tomorrow morning. Could I come with a lorry and some of my team at 10.30 am?" Roger could hardly say no.

"That would be fine."

Polly got up and the men followed. She said,

"Goodnight. Hopefully we will meet at breakfast."

Polly and Dick left to find their compartment. Roger and Chris sat down and had several more brandies.

When they got back to their carriage, Dick teased her,

"You were a little firebrand tonight. Well done. I think you will get the best out of those two."

"Were you angry with me?"

"Not at all. He deserved it."

"He annoyed me even before he came out with that racialist remark. He thought he was God's gift to women."

"I hope he has not totally put you off men tonight?"

"Come on you randy sod. I will lie on my back and let you have your wicked way with me."

In fact that is not what happened and their love making was rather energetic. Polly was worried that it had been too much for Dick. He was soon asleep. She lay thinking how she longed for attitudes to change in the world and in Kenya in particular.

Polly and Dick had finished a good breakfast, when they were joined by Chris who told them Roger was too hung over to face breakfast. Chris said he hoped he would feel better once they got to Nairobi, as they had to meet the Managing Director in the morning. Chris seemed OK and tucked into his breakfast. When they all had finished he gave Polly directions to their depot and said, even if Roger was not up to it, he would be there to meet her team, when they arrived.

What he had not expected was that Polly would be arriving with several of the hunting staff. Also as they arrived the managing director drove in behind Polly's lorry. Chris was even more worried, when Polly jumped down off the back of the lorry and hugged the managing director saying,

"Hello Uncle Peter. Your executives have been most helpful to me."

Peter Forsyth looked at Chris and replied,

"I'm glad of that Polly. What has Chris managed to do for you?"

"Chris is going to help me with the export of my game animals and he has also given me a whole lot of old gin containers to carry water in. I see them stacked over there. I know you have important meetings, so I won't hold you up." Peter Forsyth replied,

"Well done Chris. Thank you for helping my niece. Right we had better get on with the meeting. It's a pity Roger has a tummy bug, but I'm sure you can brief me about what is happening in Mombasa." He walked into the warehouse and Chris followed. All the Nairobi Staff were gathered upstairs in the small conference room. They were sitting with their backs to the large expanse of glass. This window looked out on to the large lorry park. All the windows were open to let in the very pleasant breeze. The meeting got underway.

Outside there was a large amount of African laughter. Chris could not understand any of the conversation, as it was in various tribal languages. He could recognise Polly's voice chipping in. He could not get her out of his mind. Her shorts had shown off her wonderful legs. He thought she must be a hell of a girl to work with a team of Africans. He was surprised that her father who he had assumed was Dick allowed her such a free rein. Chris, like so many men, had not noticed her engagement ring.

His attention was suddenly brought back to the room by the Managing Director saying,

"I want you to all to stand up and see an example of how to get the most out of your junior staff. I know she is my niece and therefore I'm very biased, but there she is helping to load a lorry. They are all laughing and smiling. I know some of you speak good Swahili, but she is talking in their tribal language." One of the African executives said,

"She is amazing. She is switching between Kikuyu and Wakamba. If I could not see her I would think she was a young Wakamba girl." Peter Forsyth added,

"You probably know her mother was my sister and died in childbirth. Her father was a very successful professional hunter, until he was killed by a buffalo eighteen months ago. She now runs the business which has branched out into game trapping. I must congratulate Chris from Mombasa, as he has persuaded her to let the company do her work after the animals reach Mombasa for shipment overseas." Chris was too surprised to even smile. His lasting memory of the morning was the image of an enormous African posting Polly high up into the lorry and her shrieks of laughter, as she was caught by two other Africans. The lorry had long since departed, before the meeting had finished. He wished he had had the chance to say goodbye to her.

He was pleased, when he received a note from Polly thanking him for the drums and saying she would contact him in Mombasa, when she had more details of the shipment. He was even more pleased, when he received promotion to head of section in Mombasa. Roger also got promotion, but was transferred to Mwanza on Lake Victoria in Tanzania which was certainly not a desirable posting.

Chapter 15

The Japanese shipment

Polly was sad, when Dick had to move back to Kabete, as his sick leave was over and he needed to go back to work. However she was really busy with the Japanese shipment and the preparation for the construction of the quarantine facility on Mombasa Island. Gideon volunteered to go down to Mombasa and supervise the construction. Polly went down with him in the lorry with some of the staff and some of the stores they would need. She took Gideon unannounced to Chris's office. She noticed, as she knocked that he had got promotion by the new sign on his door. Chris seemed delighted to see her. She congratulated him on his promotion. He blushed and said, he thought that her work that she had given to the company had helped. Polly introduced Gideon and enquired after Roger. She made a face, when Chris told her about his move to Mwanza. Chris added that Roger had picked a bad morning to have a hangover. He also told Polly about Peter Forsyth showing her as an example of how to get the best out of junior staff. It was Polly's time to blush.

Polly was tired, when she got back from Mombasa, as she only had one night there and came back on the lorry. They had taken a Long Wave Band Radio down to Mombasa, so they had a good means of communication. There was up to an hour's delay for telephone calls. Gideon gave her a whole list of stuff he needed.

She gave Dick a call and asked herself to lunch after she had bought all the stores. When she arrived at his house, Dick was home to greet her. He suggested that she could send Noah back to her house with the stores. She could come with him in the afternoon to CAIS and then he would run her back to her home after work. She said that was a great plan. After Mobia had brought in their lunch, Polly gave Dick a cheeky grin.

"I see it is a very light lunch my guess is that you had plans for, 'a bit of that'." She made a gesture with her forearm of a bull serving. Dick replied innocently,

"It never entered my head."

"Richard Brendon, you are so transparent. Come on eat up!"

She soon hustled him into his bedroom, much to Mobia's amusement. Suddenly she realised that Dick had taken control. She had been pushed on to her front on his bed and he was kissing the back of her neck which he knew she loved. While she was distracted she felt her knickers being pulled off under her skirt. Normally she liked him to be gentle and slow with loving her, but today she was as eager as he was. In fact they had time for a quick shower together before walking over to the CAIS.

Dick did not need much persuading to stay the night. When they got into bed at her home, Polly teased him,

"Have you been practising taking girls knickers off? You had my knickers off rather quickly at lunch."

"I must admit I do take yours off, rather often in my dreams."

"Does it turn you on to take my clothes off? I don't want to be boring by coming to bed naked." He kissed her,

"I can assure you that you are never boring."

They spent rather a long time with their love making that night, but they slept well and after a good breakfast they were ready to face the day.

Polly had good news from Gideon in Mombasa. All the pens were now ready at the quarantine station. It was time for Polly to organise the train shipment. She had already organised an area at Athi River Station so that Noah could start ferrying the animals there, so that they were very near to the railhead. Gideon brought the majority of the staff back from Mombasa to help. They had to transfer each animal into its travelling crate from its home pen on the ranch. This then had to be moved up a ramp on to the lorry, driven to Athi River and then off loaded again. There was a large amount of very hard heavy work.

Polly was not certain Miss Burrows from the 'High School' would approve of her rather scanty attire. It was very hot work. Polly decided that she would hire a crane for the actual loading of the train. She had many friends now who worked for the 'East African Railways and Harbours Company' (EAR&H Co), but she knew that, when all the flat cars arrived at Athi River and the train was booked, the EAR&H Co would want the train to move off on time. The majority of the three hundred and ten miles of track from Mombasa to Nairobi was single track, so the logistics even with the small number of freight trains was not simple.

Gideon and Noah had much better spatial awareness than Polly, so she did not interfere with the arrangements for the small crates containing the smaller animals which were going to go down on the lorry. Gideon would travel with them and Polly would travel on the train. Polly made sure that Hak came with her on the train. She smiled, as Gertrude was also on the train as cook. The two girls were not pleased that they had to remain with Hak's first wife and continue to go to school.

While they were waiting in camp at Athi River Station, Dick came over. He had brought his motorbike in the back of his Landrover so that in the morning he could go to work on it. Polly could then borrow his Landrover, so if there were problems with the animals on the train, she had some transport which was four-wheel drive and could get near to the railway track.

They tried to make love on Polly's small camp bed. It started to make alarming groaning noises. They ended up on a mattress on the ground. Polly teased Dick as, when he climaxed, he sounded very like the bed groaning. She was sad, when he roared off on the bike in the morning, as she knew she would not see him for some time.

The first setback came at Sultan Hamud about seventy miles from Nairobi. The steam train, in fact there were two of them, had the first call on the water for their steam boilers. There was not enough water for the animals. Polly had to drive a very over-laden Landrover with gin barrels full of water several times from the local dam to the train. She got quite proficient at rolling the barrels which, when full, weighed, three hundred pounds. When her Uncle had watched her in Nairobi she had been throwing empty barrels which were a much easier task.

Polly also had to help moving the fodder and the hard food to the animals, as it was being transported on two flat cars at the rear of the train. She was doing this at 4.00 am in the morning on a siding at Emali which was near to Sultan Hamud, when she heard a shout in Wakamba,

"I can see you, young Wakamba girl. You don't fool me covered in white wash." It was the stoker on the passenger train on its way to

Nairobi. He shared a cold coke with her which she was sure he had pilfered from the buffet car.

Polly enjoyed the journey through Tsavo Game Park, as her animal train came through the park in daylight, where the majority of the trip on the passenger train, through the park, was in the dark. They came through several large herds of elephants. They did not seem frightened by the train. She guessed they were very used to trains. She wondered if she would ever have to transport these magnificent animals which would weigh several tons.

It was with real relief, when she arrived safely in Mombasa. Gideon and Chris were there to greet her. Chris had helped Gideon to hire a crane, so unloading was swift. Polly was being charged by the day for the use of the flat cars, so it was vital that they off loaded as quickly as possible.

She invited Chris for supper in their camp. Much to his delight, she was having a shower in a small hessian shower tent, when he arrived. She came out to greet him wrapped in her towel. She teased him saying she was not worried about having a shower in her camp, but she would definitely lock the door if she was having a shower in the Smith Mackenzie Mess. Chris took the tease in good heart.

He had news of the freighter which he had booked to take the animals to Japan. It was waiting outside of Kilindini Harbour for a chance to come in and off load its cargo of Japanese cars. In the morning Polly joined Chris at Likoni which was near to the mouth of the harbour. They went in a bum-boat out to the freighter to meet the Captain who was Danish, but he spoke very good English. He was delighted that Polly would be sailing with her animals. He showed her the cabin that she would have. Polly made Chris smile as she whispered that she would definitely lock the door, when she had a shower.

The Captain was very hospitable and insisted that they met his officers and had a drink even though it was only ten o'clock in the morning. The drinks consisted of Danish beer and 'Aquavit' shots. Polly was very careful. Chris was not so careful. He got very drunk, but in a totally benign manner. Polly eventually steered him up on to the deck and along to the ladder above the bum-boat. She shinned down ahead of him correctly facing the side of the freighter, when she got to the bottom of the ladder she watched the bum-boat. It

121

came up on a wave and she dropped elegantly into the boat. Chris shook hands with the captain, turned and started to climb down looking out to sea. He missed his footing. The bum-boat was in a trough of a wave and so was not that close to the freighter. Chris went straight down into the water. The cold sea water had a very sobering effect and Polly had no problems hauling him into the boat.

When they got back to Likoni, Polly made sure Chris was happy to drive himself back to the 'Smith Mackenzie Mess'. As she said goodbye she gave him a peck on his cheek and said,

"Don't look so worried. I won't tell my Uncle that story, until you have got your next promotion."

A very relieved Chris drove off waving out of the window of his car.

It was a very happy camp with all the animals on Mombasa Island. They did not seem to mind the heat. Polly knew it would be several days before they could load the animals, as first of all the freighter had to dock. Then it had to off load its cargo of cars, before it was ready to take on its cargo of her animals. Chris had told her that the holds would be full of Kenyan Tea from Kericho and Kenyan Coffee from Limuru. Some of the fodder and the hard food for her animals would also be in the hold, but most of the fodder would have to be stored on deck under tarpaulins until the animals had eaten it. Polly had stressed to the Captain the need for plenty of clean drinking water.

On the third morning, Polly was doing her rounds of the animals. She loved talking to them and now that they were so much tamer she enjoyed rubbing their heads and fondling their ears. Hak came running to her to say that there was an American at the gate who had come to see her. Hak was amused, as he told Polly that the American was as black as he was. Polly had a joke with Hak, reminding him that she was just a young Wakamba girl covered in white wash.

The American introduced himself as Kirk Magruder. He was enormous. Polly was sure he was six foot and eight inches tall. He was also very well muscled. He was the agricultural attaché at the US Embassy in Nairobi. He was down in Mombasa to inspect the American aid projects in the Coast Province. He said that he had called to carry out a preliminary inspection of the quarantine facility.

He told Polly that he was not a vet, but if he was happy, a vet would be sent out from America. Polly made a long face and said,

"Won't that be very expensive?" Kirk smiled,

"For a girl as pretty as you, I'm sure my government will foot the bill!" Polly laughed,

"I don't get many complements like that, particularly, when I am in my working clothes. I do scrub up better! Can I be really cheeky and ask if you play American Football? My fiancé plays English rugby. He is quite a big guy, but nothing like as big and strong as you." Kirk laughed,

"I used to play back in the states. I went to Stanford and did a tour with the Marines before getting this job. Do you and your fiancé live in Nairobi? I would love to invite you both to one of our parties at the embassy." Polly laughed,

"I will scrub up for that!"

Gideon joined Polly to show Kirk around the quarantine. Kirk seemed impressed. Polly told him he was lucky to have come just before this shipment to Japan, as otherwise the station would be empty and there would just be a couple of watchman looking after it. They gave him some lunch and he promised to keep in touch with them.

At last Polly was given the all clear by Chris that the freighter was ready to be loaded. Gideon and Noah drove the Landrovers. They took the smallest animals first. Polly had a much bigger team which included Hak. She drove the lorry. She was pleased that Chris turned up at the quarantine station to help. She thanked him, as she knew most men in his position would have stayed in their air conditioned offices.

At the docks they used the freighter's derricks, as in fact even the largest antelope were not that heavy, relative to other cargoes. Polly was well aware that speed was necessary, as the longer they were at the berth the more the freighter had to pay. However she was adamant that the welfare of the animals was paramount.

Towards the end of the loading the PVO arrived. He had to inspect all the animals and issue health certificates. Polly knew that the conditions which the Japanese Veterinary Authorities were not nearly as stringent as the conditions which the Americans had demanded. This whole exercise was a useful trial. Polly was quite

123

touched, because, as soon as the loading was complete, only the members of her team who were travelling with the animals could remain on board. The others all stayed on docks to cheer and wave them goodbye. Gideon was now in charge. He would leave the Quarantine Station clean and tidy with two watchmen. He would then return to the ranch at Athi River. He would start making the travelling crates for the American shipment. No actual capture would start until Polly returned.

Polly had given him another task which was to design and build various sizes of squeeze crates. They both knew that the animals in the American shipment would have to be handled twice to have at least two lots of blood collected for testing for FMD.

Chapter 16

Polly has a trip to Japan

As the freighter cruised slowly out of Kilindini Harbour, Polly had very mixed emotions. She was sad to leave Dick and her beloved Kenya, but she was excited at visiting Japan. She had never been out to the Far East. She had no idea what to expect. She was apprehensive for the welfare of her animals, not only on the journey, but also in their new home in Yokohama Zoo. At least they had a very short journey, when they reached Japan, as the freighter was destined to dock in Yokohama Harbour.

There was very little wind and so the sea appeared to be calm, as they passed Likoni. Polly was grateful, as she thought rough weather would have worried the animals. In reality it was her Kenyan colleagues who were affected. The animals did not seem to be concerned, as the boat started to pitch and roll, when they reached the open sea.

Polly knew she was a 'good sailor', as she had been on various boats with her father during her childhood. However she was soon suggesting to her team that they went to their cabins and lay down. All the animals had food and water. Polly did a round of the cabins. There were four double cabins for the eight men. All eight, including Hak felt ill. Polly advised them to lie down and not to eat anything. She suggested they just had sips of water. Each cabin had a small bathroom. This contained a lavatory, a basin and a shower. She told them all that if they felt sick they must be sick into the lavatory, not into the basin. She could imagine them blocking the basin drains, and then there would be a real mess.

When she went around the cabins after she had supper with the captain she was pleased that they all seemed to be asleep. She smiled to herself. It was lucky she was not frightened of hard work. She knew it was likely that she would be feeding all the animals on her own in the morning. She checked that they all had food and water and went to her cabin. She had a shower and soon was in bed. She hugged her pillow and thought of Dick. She was soon asleep.

It was still dark at 5.00 am, when the kind steward brought her a cup of tea. She got up immediately and went on deck. The First Officer saw her and turned on the deck lights. She started feeding. She gave them all their short feed. The dawn had broken, when she started on the watering. The kind steward saw that she was in a muddle and brought her a bacon roll. She gave him a kiss on his cheek. He laughed,

"If you feel faint, you can always fall into my arms." Polly laughed,

"Dream on, but a big thank you for this 'on the move' breakfast."

Polly kept on working. Once she had finished the watering she made a quick check on the cabins. All her team were lying down, looking very grey. It really wasn't very rough, but she did remember from her school history that Lord Nelson was always confined to his cabin for three days, when he first went back to sea after a break on land. She had managed to get forage to over half the animals, when the steward suggested it would be sensible for her to stop and join the Captain for lunch. Polly realised that this was prudent, as she was feeling a little light-headed.

As she tucked into her lunch with gusto, the Captain teased her,

"I thought you white Kenyans just sat around while the black Kenyans did all the work." Polly took the teasing in the spirit in which it was meant.

"You are right with some folk, but that has never been my family's way. My father always worked harder that any of his staff. I am out of the same mould. All my team are good guys. They will come back to work as soon as they can. I think it is best if they stay in their cabins. We don't want them vomiting all over the place. I will manage. Do you mind if I work in my bikini?" He smiled,

"I will enjoy that. I will have to find my very powerful binoculars, when I am on the bridge! Would you like some of my crew to help you?"

"That is a kind offer, but I will manage for now. If I have to bring fodder up from the hold, I may well take you up on that kind offer."

After lunch she set too again. As she had started with the biggest animals, she was quicker with the forage with the smaller antelope.

Mucking them out was actually easier at sea, as she just had to chuck the muck over the side of the boat. She had enough time to have a couple of hours sitting in the sun before she had to start on the evening rounds. She had a shower before joining the Captain for supper. She liked him and he obviously liked her. Apparently it was traditional that the Captain ate alone and the officers ate as a group. He therefore was doubly glad of her company. He told her that the officers occasionally invited him to join them, but it was normally only about once a week. He teased her saying,

"I saw you in your bikini. You have such a good figure. I expect the officers will be asking you to join them every night of the week! I see you have a ring on your finger. Was that young man who came on board in Mombasa, your fiancé?"

"No, he is just a chap I have got to know from organising the shipping. My fiancé is a vet who lives and works in Nairobi. I know he would have loved to have come on this trip, but he could not get the time off. I miss him. You would like him."

"Well I will enjoy your company. You must not work too hard. I expect it will take about three days for your chaps to come back to work. Then you must have a rest. That is the Captain's orders!"

The Captain was right. Hak started work on the third morning. He was pretty weak. The others were up the next morning and they were all fine by the following day. Polly was pleased, as the animals seemed more relaxed, when the staff they knew, were about. She had been rushing so much that she had not had time to pet the animals or give them titbits.

Then the voyage became really quite restful. The weather was lovely. There was a wind, but the skies were blue. When Polly was not feeding and talking to the animals she lay on a tarpaulin in a lifeboat sunbathing and looking at the ocean. It reminded her of deep sea fishing with her father. She did actually see a sail fish leap out of the water. She also saw several different species of shark which followed the boat. The refuse from the animals attracted small fish and these then attracted, sharks and barracuda.

Hak and the other animal keepers had lost a bit of weight, when they had not eaten for three days. Polly was pleased that they were soon in good health again. She enjoyed spending time with the Captain. She learnt some Danish. He often tried and failed to get her drunk at supper. He laughed, when she explained what she had meant when she said,

"You are a very naughty man. I know you are trying to get in my knickers." Their banter was always good humoured. The nights, when they ate with the officers were a little stilted. They did not speak very good English and they rather annoyingly always were competing for her attention. She preferred just eating with the Captain.

Towards the end of the voyage the Captain warned her they were in for some rough weather. A typhoon had been forecast. They were in the South China Sea.

Polly and Hak with the help, not only of the other seven members of their team, but also some of the freighters crew, secured extra tarpaulins to protect the animals. The crew found some extra heavy chains to anchor the crates to the deck.

Polly was amazed at how quickly the tempest built up. The Captain sent word that anyone who went out on deck had to wear a lifeline. Polly was summons to the bridge. She smiled as the Captain personally wanted to check her lifeline. She told him,

"I suppose it is worthwhile letting you have a grope, if it saves me being lost at sea!"

"I think I will make it the ship's policy that you visit my cabin every morning." She replied,

"Dream on Captain, but your crew have been really helpful with the animals, so I will give you all a view of me in a kimono which I hope to buy in Japan."

However although Polly was worried about the animals, they did not seemed too stressed. Also she thought under these severe conditions that she might feel sea sick. She did not feel at all unwell and nor did any of her team. They obviously had adapted well. Mercifully the storm abated as quickly as it had come and soon the sky was blue again. As a joke she wore her lifeline, when she joined the Captain for supper. She said,

"I thought you might enjoy taking my lifeline off?" The Captain guffawed,

"Polly, you have stolen my heart. If you ever need any help anywhere, you only have to get word to me and I will help you."

He said no more, but Polly was quite touched. She knew that he really meant it. She would be a little sad at the end of the voyage.

She had little time to be sad as she had a lot to do, when they arrived. A Japanese vet came on board with the pilot, before they entered the harbour. He spoke very little English. Polly was relieved that there were duplicates of all the forms in English. Obviously the Kenyan forms which she had been given by the Game Department and the PVO were not in Japanese. However the vet seemed happy just to take a copy away. He was very thorough and looked at all the animals carefully. He had done his homework, as he brought a book which showed pictures of African animals with a description in Japanese.

He tried to explain to Polly that he was a vet who worked for the government. He said that she would meet another vet soon who worked for the zoo. This vet was not allowed on board. The boat had to dock and clear customs. Then the vet and the zoo keepers were allowed to see the animals.

This all took a considerable amount of time. Polly and her team continued to feed the animals as normal. They just had to put the muck into bags. When they eventually docked Polly could see they had a problem. The cranes which they were going to use were incredibly tall. The animals would be swung on a very high pendulum. Polly thought they would be terrified. She stopped them from starting to unload and went to see the Captain.

The Captain explained to Polly that he had no jurisdiction on the cranes. Polly remembered the instructions from her father in his will. She smiled,

"If you personally fit me into a harness, I will ride strapped to the door of the crates of the large animals to reassure them. The smaller animals will be OK as we can shut their doors and they will not have the same fear."

The Captain agreed and soon he was up on deck with his hand on some inappropriate part of her body. Hak was frightened for Polly, but she was in her element and was soon high aloft above Yokohama docks. The male eland had gone first. He was happy to be given titbits. Once he was safely on a lorry on the docks, Polly had to run to get up the gangplank so that they could hoist up the female eland. The female eland was soon with the male on the lorry. Then Polly just unhooked herself off the eland crate and hooked herself on to the hook from the crane. The crane driver was quick-witted, he immediately realised what she wanted, as she gave the thumbs up sign which obviously, Polly realised, is known throughout the world. She was up in the air flying back to the ship. The Captain was guffawing. Hak looked very worried and he reminded Polly of what he looked like at the start of the voyage.

Polly's flying continued. She thought, '*I wonder what Miss Burrows would be most upset about? I think it would be that I have not got on the regulation PE kit. I am not wearing those dreadful, thick, green pants.*'

The Japanese were very efficient; there were queues of lorries waiting for the animals. When Polly arrived with the male topi, she was greeted by a Japanese girl who explained that she was the zoo vet. Polly was delighted as, although she loved Dick, she was sure girl vets would be more caring. The zoo vet's name was Rin. She appeared rather stern, but Polly knew that smiling does not come easily to Japanese people. When Polly went to fly back to the ship, Rin held on to her, as she was frightened that she would fall. One of the Japanese stevedores explained to Rin what had happened before. It was only then that she would release Polly. She then put her palms together and bobbed her head. Polly thought she was offering up a prayer for her safety.

It was only when they were unloading the smaller animals that Rin and Polly got a chance really to talk. She insisted that Polly came to stay with her at the zoo. She said that Polly's team could easily stay in the accommodation which they had for visiting students.

It was a long day and Polly was glad to get all her animals safely to the zoo. She could tell that her team were tired, but still excited about coming to a different country. She showed them, where she was staying with Rin, if they needed her in the night.

As it was Polly got very little sleep. The zoo had a pregnant lioness that could not seem to be able to give birth. They could see blood and slim coming from her vulva, but there were no signs of a cub. Polly watched as they lured the lioness into a separate cage which was really a squeeze box, like the ones she hoped Gideon was making back home.

Once they had the lioness well secured, they put a thin strong rope around her left hind leg and pulled it out below the lowest bar of the cage. Rin then injected an anaesthetic into the vein which was easy to see on the outside of the lioness's hock, after they had trimmed away the hair. The lioness roared, but only tried to struggle, when she felt the needle prick. She was soon sleeping.

Having washed her hands and her right arm, Rin managed with plenty of lubricant to get her small hand into the vagina of the lioness. She drew out a large dead male cub. Polly was fascinated to watch. They then gave the lioness an injection of pituitary hormone which would make the uterus contract.

Polly ran to the student hostel. Hak was still awake, although it was past midnight. He came back with Polly. Polly had known that he would be interested to see a lioness giving birth. Sadly no cub was passed, and so Rin had to draw out another cub which was also dead. Rin could feel a third cub which is the normal number for a lioness, but she could not reach it, to pull it out. The lioness was given some more pituitary hormone, but still Rin could not get the cub. Rin then got her staff to start getting ready to perform a caesarean section.

Polly whispered to her,

"Would you like Hak to try to get the cub? He has very small but strong hands."

Hak washed his hands and arm carefully, but he could not manage to draw out the cub. Then Hak spoke to Polly in Wakamba.

"Can Rin find some strong thick fishing nylon with an eighty pound breaking strain?"

This was soon found and then Hak made a noose and then inserted it over his lubricated fingers into the vagina. He managed to get the noose over the head of the cub and drew it tight. Then pulling on the nylon which was wrapped around his hand he managed to draw the cub out. Rin clapped her hands together with delight. The lioness was then given an injection of antibiotics, placed in her normal cage and left to recover from the anaesthetic. The anaesthetic which Rin had used was not one which had an antidote unlike the drugs that Polly used for darting.

It was past 1.30 am, when they all eventually got to sleep. They were all very sleepy in the morning. However there was good news. The lioness was awake and had drunk some water. Polly was also pleased that all her animals were well and did not seem fazed by their new surroundings.

After all the feeding and watering had been done they stopped for some breakfast. This was some raw fish marinated in lemon juice with warm rolls. Polly liked it and thanked Rin. Rin gave her a very shy smile. Polly also liked the tea which was very different from Kenyan tea.

Rin then took Polly and the Kenyans on a tour of the zoo. It was much larger than Polly had expected. There was a large area of savannah type pasture with acacia trees which was going to be the home of the Kenyan animals, once they had acclimatised. Polly knew she would be sad to leave her animals, but she steeled herself. It was all part of her new profession. At least she was not killing them to have their heads on some wall!

The Kenyans seemed to get on well with their Japanese counterparts. Polly was interested, as over half of the zoo's labour force was girls or older women. Polly knew it would be difficult in Kenya, where there was so much unemployment, but she was determined to have more ladies in her work force at home. She thought Gertrude would definitely be a role model for other Kenyan ladies.

Rin was kind to all the Kenyans. She arranged a day's sightseeing which included a time for shopping. Polly bought a kimono which she knew Dick would love, as it had a slit up one side almost to her waist. She wore it when she went on her own to say goodbye to the Captain of the freighter. Polly could see he was close to tears, when he hugged her.

The three days went by very quickly. Polly was now keen to return to Dick and so was not nearly so sad leaving the animals, as she thought she would have been. They all seemed very happy in their new home. Rin came with them to the airport. She promised to try to come on a trip to Kenya. Polly had made another very good friend.

Chapter 17

Home again

Both Gideon and Dick were at the airport, in the early morning, when they arrived back in Kenya. They all went back to the ranch. They had some breakfast. Gideon and his team had been working hard. They had also got everything ready to go on a capturing safari, so Gideon set off in the lorry down to their camp near the Masai Mara so that they could start capturing in the morning. Polly was going to bring down Hak and the others in the Landrover after she had sorted herself out. The sorting out included a romp with Dick which they both enjoyed. He had to shoot off to work, but he promised to come down to their camp in three days, as he had some blood testing to do in Masailand.

Gideon had left Noah to drive the Landrover, as he knew Polly would be tired after her flight. However seeing Dick, and getting home, had invigorated her, so she let Noah drive, but used the journey to open her mail. She separated out the bills, so that she could pay them, when she was in the camp and send the envelopes home with the first lorry load of animals. She was pleased, as the mail included an order for game from a zoo in Germany. Polly knew that she would never get an order from the UK, as their import regulations were too strict. However she hoped that she might eventually be able to use the Mombasa Quarantine Station to export animals to Switzerland and then quarantine them there, before eventually sending them to the UK. She had to establish her reputation first. She hoped that the export to America would help.

Also in the post was an invitation from The American Ambassador asking her and Dick to a party at his residence? She knew this must be Kirk's doing. If the capturing went well she would be finished in time to return to the Athi River Ranch, and attend. She hoped that Dick would be free. She would try to contact him on the radio to give him as much notice as possible.

They all settled down into the camp routine. Polly had put Gertrude on to the payroll. She was a great asset and seemed to mother them all. Her two children were very happy now with Hak's older wife who remained on the ranch, and who made sure they went to school with all the other children. Gertrude prepared the food for all of them in the camp and they all ate together. There was a happy air about the place. The capturing went well and soon Noah had a load of animals to take to the ranch.

Dick came to see them. At supper they discussed whether they should blood test all the animals, before they even moved them to Mombasa, as if they had high antibodies against FMD it would be unlikely that they could go to America. However they decided that the handling, to blood test them, would be very stressful for the animals and expensive for Polly. If things did not work out, Polly would have to find other less lucrative places for them to be exported to.

That night Dick and Polly did not worry about a camp bed. Polly had brought a mattress down and they made love on that on the ground. Surprisingly they both slept very well and were on top form in the morning. Polly was pleased that Dick did not have to go away on safari and therefore they both could go together to the party at the American Embassy.

When they packed up the camp to come home, everyone was pleased, as the capturing had gone well. They still had more animals to capture, but they were all species which were found much nearer to the ranch. While they were camped in Masailand word must have got out that they were interested in giving homes to orphans. Thus they took home with them two very tame young Impala and four little Dikdik. Polly hoped that they would breed in captivity. She could then sell their offspring in subsequent shipments.

They continued capturing, when they got back to the ranch. Polly had a lot to do organising the permits from the Game Department. The local ranchers were very happy to sell off some of their game animals, as it brought them in much needed cash and freed up more land for breeding cattle. The DVS had managed to get countries in the Persian Gulf to take Kenyan Beef, so there was an increasing demand for good quality cattle to come into the Athi River slaughterhouse.

On the night of the embassy party, Polly and Dick had agreed that she would come to his house and then she would change there. They both could come in one Landrover to the party.

Polly arrived early and had a luxurious bath, having been given tea and cake by Mobia. Dick, unusually for him, was not late. He was most impressed with the kimono. Just as they were going out the door he slipped a hand up the slit, saying,

"Just thought I would check to make sure you had remembered to wear some knickers." Polly laughed,

"Actually they are a very, pretty, red pair which goes well with the red in the kimono. Look you can check that I'm not wearing a bra." She raised her arms and Dick got a tantalising glimpse of a beautiful breast. They were on top form when they arrived at the Embassy. Dick parked well away from the entrance, as there seem to be a large number of very smart cars which kept arriving. The cars swept up to the portico steps to deposit their passengers, before the chauffer drove off to park.

As they were nearing the steps a large Toyota limousine dropped off a Japanese couple. The man was wearing trousers and a blazer like Dick, but his partner was wearing a kimono. Polly could not resist the challenge and called out in Japanese,

"Good evening, how are you." Polly was delighted with the amazed looks on their faces. They were obviously used to Western culture, as they smiled, when they saw Polly's kimono. They asked in English,

"How do you know some Japanese?"

Polly explained that she had visited Yokohama recently to deliver some game animals to the zoo. The Japanese man introduced himself as Hiroshi and his much younger wife as Mio. Polly guessed that she was her age, but the man was older than Dick. With a cheeky grin Polly said,

"Should I call you your Excellency, as my guess is that you are the ambassador? I'm Polly and this is my fiancé Dick."

The ambassador obviously had a sense of humour, because he laughed and said he was the ambassador. However he bowed to Polly and said as she was so beautiful and was wearing a traditional Japanese costume that he was very happy to be called Hiroshi. The four of them moved to the side so they could chat together without blocking the way for other guests to climb the steps up to the very imposing front entrance. Mio asked,

"What is a fiancé? Is he not your husband? I saw him put his arm around you. In Japan only a husband would be allowed to do that!" Polly replied,

"It really means that I am betrothed to him. He has asked me to marry him and I have said yes. We hope to get married. However, we are really Kenyans rather than Europeans; therefore he should pay my father a bride price of many cows. Sadly my father has been killed by a buffalo and so I have just let him get away with buying this ring. I think I will ask Hiroshi to look after me as Dick is so naughty."

Mio said,

"I only said he would not be allowed to put his arm around you in Japan. I am sure it is allowed here in Kenya." Polly answered with a very stern face,

"What he is not allowed to do, but he did, is to put his hand through the slit in my kimono and check that I had not forgotten to put on some pants!" Both Hiroshi and Mio looked horrified. Then Polly laughed and they realised it was a joke. Hiroshi managed a little smile and Mio giggled. She added,

"I think you are both just right for one another. I think you are both equally naughty. You are very well matched like Hiroshi and me. We are both more serious, but that does not mean we do not love one another. I can assure you Dick I would never forget to put on a pair of pants and therefore my husband has no need to check." Dick then laughed,

"Now that we know we are all presentable, I think we should make our way in to meet our hosts."

There was a very tall Masai man wearing a red dress coat who was Master of Ceremonies. Hiroshi lent towards him and gave their names and said that he was the Japanese Ambassador. The Masai made a brave attempt and correctly introduced them as his Excellency the Ambassador of Japan and his lady wife. They stepped forward to shake hands with the American Ambassador and his wife. Polly lent forward and said to the Masai in his language.

"This moran is called Dick and I am called Polly. He can't take me as his bride, as he has not got enough cows for my bride price." A wide smile came on the Masai's face as he announced.

"His Excellency the Ambassador of Masailand and his hopeful wife, Polly!" The Ambassador was silver-haired and his wife was of a similar age. He was a charming man. He asked Polly,

"Why are you his hopeful wife? You are very beautiful." Polly curtsied,

"He can't afford my bride price." The Ambassador laughed,

"My dear, you are so beautiful that I don't think there are many in this room who could afford your bride price. Could I make your father an offer?" His wife butted in,

"Don't put up with any of his nonsense, Polly. I admire you as I think you spoke to Wellington in Masai. I can assure you that will not be forgotten in this house." She turned to Wellington, the Masai, and said in English,

"I bet a European has not spoken to you before in your language?" Wellington smiled,

"Indeed not Mam." The Ambassador's wife said,

"I hope we can have a chat later." Polly and Dick moved on into the sea of people.

They had no trouble finding Kirk, as he stood a head taller than anyone else. There were several surprised faces, when he hugged Polly and shook Dick by the hand. Polly thanked him for getting them invited. She said she had never felt so important, in her life, as she realised that she was going to be announced, when she came in. Kirk laughed. He said,

"I saw you. You must have said something funny, as you made the Old Man and his Lady laugh. Now let me get you both a drink."

Drinks in hand he led them out through some French windows on to a beautiful terrace which was only partial lit. It gave a wonderful view of the beautiful flood-lit gardens. There was a wonderful smell of exotic flowers in the air. They were on their own and free from the hubbub of the main reception area.

It was Polly's sharp eyes that saw them. There were three armed men dressed in black, climbing over the six foot wall to the left of the garden. She pointed them out to Dick and Kirk. She ran to head the intruders off. Dick and Kirk followed, but they were not as quick as her. She was not hindered by her kimono because of the slit in the side. The intruders had not seen them as they were in the semi-darkness. The men in black were crouched and moving along the far side of a low stone balustrade. On Polly's side of the balustrade was a table covered by a white cloth on which stood rows of red wine bottles and glasses. She grabbed two bottles and lent over the balustrade and hit the leader on the head. The other two raised their guns and fired at her, but they were two slow, as she ducked down behind the balustrade. They did not see Dick or Kirk who hurled themselves on to them. Dick is a big man. Kirk is enormous. The impact smashed the two men on to the flag stones. Their guns clattered out of their hands. Kirk had knocked his man out cold, but Dick was struggling with his man. The man dropped, when Polly hit him with her second bottle.

Kirk helped Dick to his feet and handed one of the guns to Polly, saying,

"I guess being a hunter you know how to work these things." He grabbed the other two guns, but took no chances and with one in each of his enormous hands he covered the unconscious men on the ground. The embassy armed askaris soon arrived together with some embassy staff who dragged the unconscious men away. Kirk relinquished the guns to two policemen who had arrived and, with an arm around each of them, walked Polly and Dick up to the residence.

The silver-haired Ambassador was on the patio to greet them.

"Thank you Kirk. You and your two friends did a mighty fine job. Polly you certainly know how to run. Dick I will make up any deficit with the bride price, even if I have to ship some of my cattle over from Texas!" Dick replied,

"She may run very fast, but I don't intend to let her run away from me, Sir."

"I'm glad to hear that. Now we must not let this little altercation spoil the party. The police suggest that everyone stays in the reception area, until they have checked out the grounds. So come in and let's get you some more drinks."

The noise in the main hall had risen by several decibels. The American Ambassador's wife came over to them. She hugged Polly to her.

"I knew you were somehow different, as soon as I met you. You must take more care, my dear, in these dangerous situations. I saw you streak unarmed across the garden to stop those armed men. You are too brave for your own good." She turned to Dick,

"You must look after her."

"I will do my best."

"Now let me introduce you to some guests. Everyone wants to meet you."

They met several other guests before they managed to get together with the Japanese couple. Mio said to Polly.

"You were amazing you were like a flash of red light. I'm surprised that your kimono did not hinder you."

"I think it is because I choose one which was slightly shorter and had a slit which came higher up. I knew Dick would like that. My time in Japan was much too short. I hope I get another chance to deliver some animals and pay your country another visit." Mio replied,

"We both love Japan, but we love the diplomatic service, as we love to travel." Then Kirk came over and said he was sorry to bother them, but the police would like a word with them about the incident.

Polly was very surprised, as they were shown into a small office in the embassy by Kirk to meet not an inspector, but the Deputy Police Commissioner. Polly knew he was a Wakamba, as he looked so like Gideon. He said, "Thank you for sparing me the time. I just wanted to thank you for your prompt action which has averted a major political incident. The perpetrators which we have arrested without any loss of life, thanks to you, are all Somali Nationals. They were intending to make a statement for the world press. Apparently the Russians have made a slaughter house in Kismayu. The Americans have made a water supply and are reluctant to allow the use of the clean water which is vital for the meat plant. The Ambassador has promised that he will bring the matter to the fore at the highest level. If my force can ever be of any help to you in the future please do not hesitate to contact me personally."

Polly could not resist replying in Wakamba,

"Thank you, Commissioner that is most kind of you." He raised his eye brows,

"I have been a policeman for over thirty years, but I have never met a young white Wakamba girl dressed as a Japanese lady. I hope we meet again." He shook their hands before they left.

Eventually Polly and Dick got back to his house. He put his arms around her.

"Now I would like to see these pretty red knickers."

"I think as you have been such a good boy tonight, you might see a lot more."

Chapter 18

The American shipment

As Polly and her team had done it before, getting all the animals down to Mombasa seemed easier and was accomplished without incident. Polly was concerned that the quarantine centre had not yet been visited and more importantly approved by the American vets. She contacted Kirk at the embassy who said that they had been waiting as the senior American Government Vet wanted the animals to be at the station. Kirk said he would Fax the USA and let her know what was happening. He was good to his word. The vet was arriving in three days. He had said it would be in order for them to start the first official blood test provided they did not plan to bring in any more animals.

Polly then was in a bit of panic. Dick came to her rescue and managed to come down so he could take the blood. The squeeze crates which Gideon had designed and got constructed were a big help, but still the animal had to be held. A noose had to be put around their neck to raise the jugular, so that a needle could be inserted. The blood was then collected into a glass bottle. It was a laborious process, as then the glass bottles had to stand in the cool to allow the blood to coagulate. When the serum had separated from the clot, it had to be drawn off with a sterile pipette. Finally the serum had to be frozen. It could then be transported to the laboratory. Dick had the excellent idea that if they could get all the samples collected then the American vet could take them back with him to America.

Polly went to the airport to collect the visiting vet. She left Dick collecting blood samples, as there were still several to take. Polly did not know what to expect. Would the vet be a youngish high flyer like Roly or would he be an old experienced man. She knew that there was a large amount of money hanging on the result of his visit. She had got up in the night leaving Dick sleeping to work out some figures. If the American shipment failed and she could not find another buyer for the animals she would be definitely be bankrupt. If

141

she could find another buyer, like a Japanese zoo then there was just a chance that she could keep going. Dick had woken, when she had got back into bed. They had gently made love. She was so thankful that she had him by her side. She thought how she could have lost him forever in Tana River District. Going bankrupt was nothing as bad as that. She had then slept soundly.

Mombasa was a very small terminal. Polly saw that the Nairobi flight had not yet landed, so she went and bought a coffee. She sat by the window. The flight arrived and Polly watched the passengers. One man ran back to the ramp and obviously had left something on the plane. He started to try to climb the ramp, while other passengers were trying to disembark. The ground staff tried to restrain him. Polly could see he was getting extremely angry. She thought, '*It will just be my luck, if he is the vet*'. Then she remembered her father's will. '*She must smile*'. She thought about Dick's gentle love making during the night. She smiled. She was still smiling went the passengers came through the arrivals gate. She held up the white card she had prepared. The passengers all filed past her just glancing at her card which read 'Floyd Moon'. Polly had that sickening feeling. The vet was the angry man. He came striding up to her. She held out her hand.

"Hello Floyd. Thank you for coming to Mombasa."

"It's Doctor Moon. Who are you?"

"I'm Polly Cavendish, thank you for coming all this way Doctor Moon to see my animals."

"I haven't come to see your animals. I've come to see the quarantine facility. We will have to wait. They won't release my brief case."

"Would you like a coffee, while we wait?"

"No. I'm surprised your Father isn't here to meet me." Polly laughed. She could not resist her bubbly nature any longer.

"I'm surprised you didn't see him up there in the sky on your flight. He was killed by a buffalo almost two years ago!" The colour drained from his face. He didn't know what to say. Polly took his arm and said,

"I think you need a stiff gin and tonic. Let me just have a word with this guy, before we go to the bar." Polly politely asked in Kikuyu, if he could bring the missing brief case to the bar. The man replied that he would be pleased to do that. Then she took Floyd's arm again,

"I'm sorry I forgot that all American vets are called Doctor. My fiancé is a vet who qualified at Edinburgh so he is just Mr."

At last Floyd relaxed,

"I'm very sorry for being so rude. I just lost it, when I realised I had forgotten my briefcase. I have never been out of the US before. I know I shouldn't say this, but I'm a bit out of my depth." Polly said,

"I will look after you. Let's face it; it is in my own interest to make sure the quarantine station passes your inspection."

The brief case arrived at the same time as the G & Ts. Polly thanked the Kikuyu man. Floyd asked,

"Was that Swahili?"

"No it was his own language which is Kikuyu. Africans are marvellous linguists they nearly all speak two tribal languages as well as Swahili. Of course many also speak English. I try to learn their language, as I feel it is only polite."

"Well thank you for getting my briefcase back so efficiently. I thought I had lost it forever."

Floyd was a totally different young man from the Mr. Angry he had been before. Polly could not say she liked him, but she no longer wanted to punch him on the nose. He told her about his home in New York. Although he was a vet, she got the impression that he was a real townie and so a job working for the Department of Agriculture was just up his street. Polly thought he was still fairly nervous, as he talked a lot, as she drove him down the causeway on to Mombasa Island. She was glad they had booked him into to the Nyali Beach Hotel, as then he would really get the impression that Mombasa was an island, as the regulations required. The causeway rather negated that Mombasa was an island. Kirk had been fine with it, but this guy might not be so easy to convince.

When they arrived, Dick was trying to bleed an Eland. Polly was worried he would get hurt. She did not want to distract him. Hak and Gideon were helping him. However she did want to warn them all, so she said in Swahili,

"This is the American vet. He has got an explosive temper. I will entertain him." She turned to Floyd,

"I don't want to distract them. I know they want to meet you, but they are a bit tied up at the moment. Let's get some of the boring stuff over with. If you would like to come with me I will show you the double perimeter fence and see if you are happy with it."

Polly led him off and started talking about America. Floyd seemed happy to come with her. Obviously the last thing he wanted to do was to have to wrestle with a bad tempered Eland. On their walk, they saw some Sykes monkey's with their long tails. Luckily they were outside of the perimeter fence, but Polly knew they did get in occasionally, to steal food. They were not very frightened of humans and hissed at Polly and Floyd. Floyd said,

"I don't like the look of them. Do they bite?" Polly replied,

"I think they would, if they were cornered, but actually they are frightened of man and run away. They have an unpleasant habit of defecating and throwing their faeces at you. I can assure you we keep them out." Mercifully he seemed happy with that. Polly was worried that she would have to spend more money on raising the height of the fence. She had thought about electrifying the fence, but did not want to add to her expenses.

To walk right around the perimeter took quite a long time. Floyd asked questions about distances. He took notes on a pad. He also had a measure which he used at intervals. When he wasn't looking Polly unbuttoned a couple of buttons of her shirt. She was wearing a bra so it was not very revealing, but she thought she might have to make some sort of distraction.

They got back to the entrance and Floyd measured the gates. Then he asked,

"I remember Kirk said in his preliminary report that there are no cloven hoofed animals on Mombasa Island. How could you prove that?" Polly's heart sank. She was going to have to do a lot more than undo a couple of buttons! She improvised, remembering to smile,

"It is a District Council bylaw. It is well policed, as the authorities are well aware that many of the populous would like to have animals, particularly goats in their gardens. The police have a large police dog section." Luckily Floyd did not ask for any more details. Then he said,

"I see quite a large number of chickens in the compound. I think they are a disease risk." Polly had not been at the 'High School' in Norwich for nothing. She gave him a big smile,

"Don't worry Floyd, if we start exporting Ostriches I will clear them out. There are such lovely wild birds in Kenya. You must come back and go on safari. I'm sure you would enjoy it."

Polly was so relieved, when they had finished all the blood collecting and Dick, Gideon and Hak came over. She introduced them. She was also delighted that Gertrude banged a gong so that they all could sit down at the long table for lunch. It reminded Polly of the hunting days, when she would have to attend to the clients every whim. She thought she had been well trained for entertaining Floyd. Floyd turned to Dick and said,

"The ambassador spoke very highly of you and Polly. His nick name for you was 'The Ambassador of Masailand'. Why was that?" Dick replied,

"You may have noticed that Polly is marvellous at speaking different tribal languages. There is a tall Masai guy who works at the embassy. Polly had a joke with him, saying 'that I could not afford her bride price." Floyd looked perplexed so Polly had to explain to him all about the buying of wives. She ended by saying,

"Have you bought a wife yet Floyd?" Floyd replied quite sharply,

"No I haven't and I don't intend to." Polly wisely did not continue the joke, as she was slightly nervous that Floyd was gay.

After lunch, Polly was relieved, as he asked to be dropped at his hotel. He said he wanted to write up his report while everything was fresh in his mind. Dick volunteered to take him. Polly was really grateful. She had rather had enough of him. They went as soon as they had finished lunch.

In the afternoon, Polly helped to suck up the serum from the final group of blood samples. She hoped that Floyd would take them, as she knew sending them couriered by airfreight would be a real mission and very expensive. She hoped Chris at 'Smith Mackenzie' might have some ideas on how to send the second batch.

When they had finished the serum collection they started on the afternoon feed. Polly noticed how all the animals were much more nervous. It only took one frightening episode in their lives to set them back weeks of gentling. When Dick got back he helped her with the feeding so that they could chat. They got very little time together.

"What did you think of Floyd?"

"He certainly is a very strange chap."

"Do you think he is gay?"

"No I don't think so. He certainly would not admit it, but I'm sure he really fancies you. He is very unsure of himself. I think he has been promoted to this job too soon. I wonder if he has got very influential parents. You are right about him being short tempered. He got cross with the receptionist at the hotel. He might even be a racist. If so they sent him on the wrong assignment."

"I hope he does not fail the quarantine. So much hangs on it."

"I agree. I am sure there is an appeal process, but I doubt if it is quick. I'm sure the DVS would give his recommendation, but that would count for very little in the USA. One good thing is that he has agreed to take the samples for us. He actually volunteered. I think he thought it would show what an important man he was. I would have hated the job, as there is bound to be problems both here in Kenya, and I suspect even more in America."

Supper was a much more relaxed meal that night. Polly was pleased as Dick had managed to swing it so he could stay the night. Sadly he had to leave early in the morning, as he needed to be back at Kabete by the afternoon. Polly got up to see him off. She kissed him passionately before saying,

"Keep safe, I love you so much."

After he had driven off in the dark she went back to bed and had a little more sleep before the camp became alive and the morning feeding started. They got it finished before all sitting down for a lovely breakfast which Gertrude had prepared. Polly loved the mangos which were called 'Lamu Mangos'. They were much bigger and sweeter than any other mangos. Polly was just getting ready to get down to some boring book work, when a taxi drew up. Floyd had sent a note.

Dear Polly

I know you said you would come over in good time this afternoon to the hotel to pick me up to take me and the

samples to the airport, but I wondered if you would like to come over this morning to discuss my report?

Kind Regards
Floyd

Polly thought with a smile. '*Perhaps Dick was correct. Maybe he does fancy me. Hopefully the report can't be too bad otherwise I don't think he would want to discuss it. It certainly is an invitation that I can't refuse.*'

She told Gideon what she was doing. They packed up the samples as that would save her coming back to the quarantine station. She could go straight to the airport. As an afterthought she put on a bikini under her clothes. When she got to the hotel she got them to put the samples into the deep freeze. She found Floyd sitting by the pool in his swimming costume. He obviously had been writing the finishing touches to his report. She said,

"I'm glad you are making the most of the sun in the time you are here. We Kenyans rather take it for granted." He did not answer, but just pushed the handwritten report over to her. Polly started to read it. He got up and walked to the pool and dived in.

The first two pages were straight forward. He just described the station and its environs. It was when she started to read his comments that her heart sank. He said that the disinfection and disease control were virtually non-existent and that under the circumstances he could not recommend the facility. She stood up and thought about her father's will. It was very difficult to smile. Slowly she took off her clothes so that she was just in her bikini. There was no one else in the pool. She walked to the pool and dived in. She knew he had been watching her. She surfaced near to where he was standing, in about five feet of water by the edge of the pool. She smiled and pulled herself up gracefully, so she was sitting on the edge of the pool. He joined her with rather a lot of splashing. She was about to tell him what a financial mess she would be in if she did not get this American export, but then the strong Polly asserted itself. She said smiling,

"I'm going to give you back your report. This is Africa. It is totally impossible to carry out the disinfection and disease control which you suggest. Anyone in the USA who has worked in Africa will know what you are recommending is totally impossible. You will be a laughing stock in your Department. Come on I will help you to rewrite your recommendations so that they are realistic." She put her hand on his shoulder to make it easier for her to get to her feet. When she was up she offered her hand to help him up. They walked over to the table. She sat opposite. His eyes kept flicking up to her breasts. Every time they went up to her face, he saw her smiling at him. He found it was very difficult to concentrate. He was very aroused. He was embarrassed, as it was very easy to see. Polly could see he was not writing so she asked,

"You seem to have got writers block. Would you like me to dictate for your?" His throat was very dry. He gulped,

"Yes please that would be very helpful." Polly started to dictate. His body had dried and now he seemed to be burning. Sweat began to pour off him. After to a few minutes Polly said,

"Come on let's have a cool off in the pool?"

"I can't move I'm too embarrassed."

"Don't worry there is no one else here. I'm not bothered."

So they had another cooling dip in the pool. He dried his hands and continued writing. After two more dips in the pool, he finished. Polly said as she wrapped her kikoi around her,

"You read it through to check on the grammar and the spelling, while I get us some drinks. When she came back, he had started making a final copy. Polly said,

"The waiter insisted on bringing the 'Tuskers'. I hope you will like them. We all tend to drink them, as they are locally brewed. I think they are a cross between a larger and an Indian Pale Ale (IPA), but I am not an experienced beer drinker. I sometimes drink a G&T, when I get worried that I might get a fat tummy." His eyes dropped to her body.

He finished the final copy and they had some lunch. Other guests had come down to the pool. When they had finished lunch, Polly said,

"You had better go to your room I will get the samples organised and then I will take you to the airport." She saw him hesitate. She smiled,

"Don't worry I will come and stand in front of you while you wrap your towel around yourself. No one will see."

"Thank you I have never been in this predicament before!"

When he had gone, Polly put on her clothes. Her bikini was still a little wet, so it wet her shirt, but she did not worry. She had retained his draft copy of the report. She folded it carefully. She was going to make sure he knew she had it. She also folded his first report.

On the way to the airport he was quiet, so Polly chatted away about Kenya and how the countryside was so variable and how they could grow such marvellous tea and coffee, as well as produce top quality beef.

Checking in the blood samples took time, but eventually his flight was called. Polly lent forward and kissed him on the cheek. Floyd said,

"Thank you for being so kind to me. I have never met a girl as beautiful as you before. I'm sorry for getting over excited." Polly smiled and said,

"Have a safe journey. Goodbye." She waved the folded up report. He shouted,

"Thank you again. Goodbye." He went to get on his flight.

She just hoped he would not forget either the samples or his briefcase and then lose his temper. He was certainly a strange character.

When the animals had all settled down, Polly and Gideon thought they would return to the ranch, leaving Hak in charge. Gertrude came back with them, as she was missing Ruth and Sita. The following day Polly was once again doing paperwork. She started on the post. There always seemed to be bills which depressed her. She was pleasantly surprised by a letter from a zoo in Bahrain. They wanted four breeding pairs of Oryx. These would not be very easy to capture, but Polly knew that she could ask a very good price. However what really excited her was that she might be able to persuade Dick to take a little of his leave and come with her on the boat. The two of them could easily look after eight animals and they could have a short relaxing holiday.

She gave Mobia a ring. He said that Dick was due home that night, but he had told Mobia not to cook or wait up, as he was likely to be late. Polly asked Mobia if he would leave the door open, as she would come over and give Dick a surprise. Mobia said he knew that Dick would like that.

Josiah gave her an early supper. She had a good shower and washed her hair. She had plenty of time for it to dry before she got into the Landrover and drove to Dick's house. The outside light was on. She checked that Mobia had left the front door open. Then she got back in the Landrover and parked it a little way up the drive to the CAIS. She had not really hidden it, but she was fairly confident that Dick wouldn't see it. She went in. Once she was in his bedroom she striped off and put on a pair of sexy pyjamas. It was quite cool so she snuggled into bed with her book. When she felt sleepy she turned off the bedside light and she was soon asleep. In fact she must have been very tired, because she did not hear his Landrover.

Dick was tired, but he was alert, he noticed Polly's scent. Just her smell lifted his spirits. He quietly opened his bedroom door and could see from the dim light in the hall the lump in his bed. He shut the door and had a shower in the spare bathroom. He realised Polly must be really tired not to hear his Landrover. He so wanted to make love to her, but he managed to resist the temptation to wake her. He got in to bed carefully. Her back was to him. She shifted in her sleep and just felt him, but did not wake. She pulled his upper arm over her and placed his hand on her breast. Dick had a wonderful sensation of feeling her breast through her silk pyjamas. He groaned with desire, but eventually went to sleep.

They both woke as Mobia brought through the tea. Polly rolled into his arms,

"Why didn't you wake me? I love you so much. Don't talk. Just take me." It was Polly's turn to groan as she felt him pull down her pyjama bottoms and enter her from behind. Their tea got cold, but at last they drank it and got up.

Over breakfast Polly confessed, how she had manipulated Floyd. She was worried that Dick would disapprove. In fact he appeared to think it was, not only very funny, but also very wise.

"It was a win, win, situation. If he had sent in that report he would have been the laughing stock of his older colleagues in the States. Equally it would have been very difficult for you to get his initial recommendations rescinded. All fair in love and war." He added with a smile,

"I assume it was war not love!" Polly blushed,

"Of course it was, you silly sod. Now I'm going to be very manipulative. I have a new request for a group of eight Oryx required in Bahrain. Could I persuade you to come with me as my only animal attendant? I thought we could have a brief holiday on the boat. Could you take the time off?"

"That sounds a great idea. I would love that. Nearer the time, when you know roughly, when the consignment is going, I will book the leave.

Polly was a very happy girl when she returned to ranch. She could not wait to capture the Oryx. The American consignment went to the back of her mind. The ranch always came alive, when there was more work. Gideon got eight transport crates big enough for Oryx to be prepared. Polly managed to get a permit from the Game Department to capture them in the Mukogodo Area of the Northern Frontier District (NFD). The Mukogodo Area lies north of the Ewaso Ng'iro River to the west of Samburu Game Park. Although it is only just in NFD it is a very dry remote area. Oryx are amazing animals in that they seem to be able to manage without water. They are one of the biggest antelope standing over four feet at the shoulder. Both sexes have long, straight, wicked horns. They are animals not to be tangled with. It is rumoured that they have killed adult male lions with their horns.

Polly knew their skin was thick enough for her to use the capture gun rather than the crossbow. She knew that getting close to them was going to be very difficult. The crossbow did have an advantage in that the bolts could carry more anaesthetic, but they also dropped more, so that Polly had to make more allowances for their trajectory.

The most direct route for them to get to the western end of the Mukogodo was to turn left before they reached Samburu Game Park, rather than crossing the Ewaso Ng'iro River at Archer's Post. The disadvantage of this shorter route was that they had to cross the Ewaso Ng'iro River at a ford, called the Barsalinga Crossing. If there had been rain up in the Mathew's Mountains the river would be too high to ford and they would have to back track which added a considerable distance to their journey. Polly opted for the shorter route, but she put on her bikini under her shorts and top in case she needed to test the depth of the water.

It took them until 5.00 pm to reach Barsalinga. Much to Hak's alarm Polly insisted that she would test out the crossing. She took off her shirt and shorts leaving her in her bikini. She kept on her gym shoe, as there might be some sharp rocks under the water. The water was full of mud and so she would have no idea what she was going to tread on. In Samburu Game Park the river is not nearly so fast flowing and so there are a few crocodiles. Luckily crocodiles do not come further up river to Barsalinga, where the water is, either too shallow for them, or if there has been rain, it is too swift flowing.

The air was still very warm. This made the chill of the river more marked. Polly gave a little gasp, when the water came over her bikini bottoms. Dick had told her that a Landrover could cross, if the water did not come above his waist. As his legs were so much longer than Polly's, she thought they could cross, if the water did not come above her bikini top.

She was crossing well until she stepped down into a hole in the river bed. She went under, but was soon up swimming well, much to Hak's relief. Although the current was swift and she was washed about fifty yards down river, she soon reached the other side. They watched her running on the bank up river. She had marked in her mind, where the hole was in the river bed. When she returned she made sure she was upriver of it and so she returned without the level coming above her breasts.

Polly always used her commonsense, so she decided to camp on the south side of the river and cross in the morning, when they had a whole day ahead of them. Before she went to bed she made a mark on a rock in the river, so she could see if the level changed in the night.

In the morning Polly could not be certain, but it looked like the river had dropped by about six inches. She was pleased, as it definitely had not risen. She was sure the lorry with its higher clearance would get across OK. When they had packed up the camp, with Polly in the water guiding them, the lorry set off. To her delight it was soon across.

Gideon took the fan belt off the Landrover to try to stop the fan splashing water over the plugs, the distributor or the coil. Then he too set off. He kept up a steady speed to make a bow-wave in front of the radiator. All went well until he was right in the middle when water must have got under the bonnet and the engine died. Polly was worried the vehicle was going to be washed away. She shouted,

"Quick everyone, Come in the water and push I will rescue you if you fall."

The majority of the staff had come across with the lorry so they had to wade back. Luckily the water only got deep for them as they got near to the stricken Landrover. One of the guys slipped as he was getting out of the Landrover. He was washed away by the current. Polly was after him in a flash. She was helped by the current and soon had his head above the water so he could cough and splutter. In his panic he grabbed her bikini top which ripped off. Polly thought, *'What the hell.'* She soon had him on the bank.

Soon the staff and a topless Polly were trying to push the Landrover. Obviously it had a wheel stuck behind a rock. Gideon shouted,

"Everyone push, when I used the battery to turn the wheels. The Landrover leapt forward and they all pushed. Several of the men fell, but they held on to the vehicle so they did not get washed away. Eventually they got the Landrover near enough to the bank for Noah to tie on a towrope from the lorry. Slowly he backed the lorry and pulled the Landrover well clear of the water.

The sun was now high in the sky. Their clothes soon dried. Polly found a shirt to put on. Gideon teased her saying,

"It's lucky Lady Standup is not on this safari!" Polly laughed,

"I have spent too long at the coast with the Giriama."

She helped Gideon dry the inside of the distributer after he had put the fan belt back on. Then, they got going and reached a good camping spot by a deep water hole, surrounded by large trees in the Mukogodo, before noon. The trackers went out immediately, while the others set up camp.

Polly was fascinated by the water hole. It was about forty feet deep. It was used intermittently by the local Samburu. There were rickety ladders about eight feet long going down in stages to the bottom. Polly climbed down. At the bottom the sand was wet. She dug into it and was rewarded by a small pool of water which, when she tasted it was sweet and not salty. They had brought quite a large volume of water in the old gin containers, but Polly knew that she would have to supervise a detail of the men to lift more water to the surface.

Towards evening time the trackers returned to say they had found some Oryx. It was a cheerful camp. The young man who had ripped off Polly's bikini top came to her rather sheepishly and apologised. Polly teased him,

"I knew you did it purposely so you could see my tits. Will they be big enough to feed Dick's babies?" He replied very seriously,

"I think they will grow bigger when you need them." Polly thought, '*I am sure Auntie Margaret would not approve of this conversation. I think he is right. I hope they won't get too big.*'

In the morning, leaving two men to guard the camp they set off after the Oryx. They had small two way radios. When they got near to the place where the trackers had seen the Oryx the day before, Noah stopped the lorry. Polly strapped herself to the top of the Landrover on the mattress and Gideon drove the Landrover. Polly smirked. She never lay on the top of the Landover strapped down without thinking of Dick. She was looking forward to their boat trip. She had no time for daydreaming, as the bush was quite thick. Although Gideon did his best, she had to avoid the thorn branches.

They soon found the Oryx there were five of them, one young male and four females. Polly would have liked to have darted the male, but he always seemed to be looking at the vehicle. She managed to hit a female in the rump. The whole herd moved off at gallop, but they soon slowed and just walked. The darted animal started to stagger and then went down. The others did not wait for it, but continued walking. Gideon summoned Noah, but continued to follow the group, leaving Hak and another man with the Oryx.

Polly managed to dart a second female. The anaesthetic must have gone into a vein in the muscle, as within a few yards the animal was down. It was agonizing waiting for the lorry. Polly was worried that it would wake up. Eventually the lorry arrived and they lifted the Oryx up into the lorry and into a crate. Polly was delighted as she managed to inject the antidote into the two animal's jugular veins at her first attempt.

They decided to keep tracking the Oryx, as although Polly was happy that the trackers would not lose them, she thought they might move several miles from the camp during the afternoon and the night. They were very successful and managed to dart and load the two remaining females before the light began to fail. Polly was sad for the male as he galloped off on his own, but she was confident that the trackers would be able to follow his spoor in the morning.

The male sniffed the scent of his females in the wind. He was perplexed. Two days earlier he had met a group of five younger males. One had challenged him to take his harem. In a mock fight, he had locked horns with the challenger and had easily thrown off his adversary. Had his females gone to join this young male? He followed the scent. It led him to Polly's camp. She was just doing a final check of the four females in their crates before going to bed.

The male Oryx was incensed. What was this animal doing between him and his females? He charged. As he neared Polly, he dropped his head and skidded to a halt. Polly did not hear him, as his hooves made little sound in the soft sand of the camp. He was directly behind her. He raised his horns up rapidly and jabbed them into her two bullocks. She screamed, as she was lifted into the air. She grabbed the top of the high crate and pulled herself up. He backed up and charged into the crate. He got his horns totally wedged into the solid wood of the crate. Polly shouted to Gideon, Hak and four other men who had come to her scream,

"Grab him." This they did after they had tied his legs. They put him in one of the crates with a female. Polly got down and hobbled towards them. Gideon said,

"Polly. You're hurt. Where did he get you?"

"You had better bring a torch and come to my tent to find out."

Polly was very sore. She lay face down on her camp bed. Gideon came into the tent she said,

"It is so humiliating yesterday I had to show you my tits today I have to show you my bottom. It is really sore can you ease my shorts off gently? They are rather snug." She reached down underneath herself and undid the buttons down the front of her shorts. As he drew her shorts down she pulled the two bows on the sides of her bikini bottoms. She sensed he was laughing quietly. She said,

"You can laugh. It's bloody painful."

"I'm sorry. I could not stop myself. It's as if someone has painted a red eye on each of your white buttocks. The eyes are very symmetrical. If only it had been an old male, his horns would have been wider and they would have missed you." Polly groaned,

"Thanks for that! If he had been a big strong male he would have smashed my pelvis. I suppose I should be grateful. I'm not going to let you touch the wounds in the poor light. I will sleep on my front and you can cover the wounds in the morning, when you can see what you are doing."

In the morning Polly could hardly move. She was much bruised. Gideon put on some ointment and a big square plaster on each wound. Polly thought, '*At least we have captured the male. There is no urgency. The trackers can go out and see if they can find a herd of young males.*'

She was like an old woman moving around the camp, she certainly could not sit down, but she could lie down. She felt very old, when three Samburu girls in their early teens arrived in the camp. No one had seen them come. They seemed to have just come from thin air. They were bare chested and had reached puberty. Soon they would get married. They said their Manyatta was quite near, but Polly guessed it was really a long way away. She had forgotten, when she had been laughing about the Giriama ladies at the Coast going without anything on their upper bodies that the Samburu and their cousins, the Rendile further north, also went bare chested. She had no need to worry about losing her bikini top. It was normal for the NFD, but she doubled if Auntie Margaret would see it that way.

The trackers returned that night, but they had not been successful in finding any oryx. Polly knew she should not be, but she was relieved that she would have a little longer to recover. She left the plasters in place, as she did not want to bother Gideon again. She did admit to herself that she was a little shy. She had known Gideon all her life, so he was like a father, but when she thought about it, she would not now be happy showing her bottom to her real father, if he had been alive.

In the morning Gideon drove out with the trackers to widen the area. They were successful and located a herd of seven young males. The capture was planned for the following morning. Polly was not so sore, but she knew she ought to change the dressings on her wounds. They were revolting and discharging pus. She washed them in disinfectant which stung a bit, but not half as much as the

156

mercurochrome which she painted on. She was stamping her foot on the ground to cope with the pain. She had tears in her eyes. She was glad no one could see her. However she was confident that the mercurochrome would dry them. She remembered her father painting it on to her knees, when she had fallen on to some coral on the Kenyan Coast. She smiled through her tears. She remembered crying then and her father wrapping her in his arms.

It was a hot night so she did not cover the wounds and slept without a sheet. In the morning the wounds seemed to be dry, but she was taking no chances. She put on three pairs of knickers under her shorts! She rather gingerly climbed on to the mattress and strapped herself down. However in her normal shooting position she was quite comfortable. They had a very successful day and darted three young males. Polly was very relieved. At the end of the day she was exhausted and could feel that pus had seeped through to her shorts. She had a good shower and put on more mercurochrome. She thought there must be an improvement, as it did not sting so much. She still wished that Dick was with her to give her a hug. She knew that in spite of her tough exterior she was still a little girl inside.

She was glad of the two more days that they had in camp to allow the oryx to settle down. She was dreading the journey home. She felt sorry for the oryx, but realised they had no imagination what was ahead of them. They were all eating OK. She marvelled that they did not drink, but of course they had water in front of them, if they needed it.

She now could sit down, provided she sat gently, but she knew sitting in the Landrover would be hell. She could see that they were very short of space for the journey home. However Gideon became aware of her problem, so they loaded the Landrover roof very carefully. The mattress and her harness were in place as normal, but they made a tunnel for her with boxes and tables so they could load more on top of her. They all thought it was a huge joke. Gideon said they would not risk the Barsalinga Crossing, but would go the longer way around through Archer's Post.

In fact the first part of the journey went well. Although the Landrover created a large amount of dust, it was not a problem as there was very little other traffic, because they had set off early in the morning. It was only when they were on the climb up from Isiolo to

Timau that there was an unbearable amount of dust. Polly banged on the top of the roof of the Landrover. When Gideon stopped she wriggled out. She drank some water and had some food, before she returned to the roof. This time she climbed up on the bonnet and wriggled into the hole so that she was facing backwards. Gideon went to the back to check that she was OK. Polly said,

"There is only one problem I can't use my harness so I'm relying on you. No big bumps or my bottom will be seriously sore." Gideon laughed,

"Dick is going to die laughing when he hears about this safari."

"He had better not or I will kill him!"

When they stopped in Nanuyki to get petrol, Polly turned around again, as they were on tarmac from then on. Eventually they reached the ranch soon after 10.00 pm. There was still a lot of work to be done, as they had to get the oryx down in their crates off the lorry and get them into to their permanent pens. Polly was really grateful to them all, as they all worked hard with a lot of laughter. When she eventually got into a nice warm shower she was appalled how dirty she was. Her knickers were absolutely disgusting. She nearly funked putting on the mercurochrome, but she steeled herself. It was quite cold so she put on some pyjamas. She did not want to make a mess on the sheets.

In the morning she was delighted as, when Josiah heard about her injuries he found a child's, blow-up, rubber ring which Polly had used, when she was four years old, when she was learning to swim. She could sit on that. She was much more comfortable.

There was also good news in the post. All the blood samples from the American shipment were negative for FMD. That night she rang Dick. Mobia told her that he was away on Safari, but hoped to be back for the rugby game on Saturday. Polly said that she would try to meet him there. She hoped her wounds would have healed up by then. Also in the post was her bank statement. Thanks to the Japanese shipment she was still in the black. She dug out Roly's old financial plan and compared it with her new figures. She was delighted that she had achieved better than Roly had planned. She also had not touched any of the cash that he was unaware of. Whether she could survive all hinged on the American Export.

She smiled to herself. '*She would not be able to save the business by selling her body now. Who would want a girl with scars? At least they were hidden by her bikini bottoms. She still might get away with it!* Then she chastised herself. '*What was she thinking about? She was engaged to Dick, but what if two holes in her buttocks repelled him. She just could not worry about it!*'

Chapter 19

Dick gets concussion

By Saturday she was walking and indeed running normally. The wounds had granulated well and were no longer infected, but Polly thought they looked gross, as they were covered by two, dry, dark brown scabs. Polly even considered covering them in make-up. Her only consolation was that they were no longer oozing and so she did not need to wear two pairs of knickers. She wore a pretty pair which matched her bra. She paid attention to her appearance and wore a dress that she knew Dick liked. She did not try to get to the pitch before the game as she knew that the 'Nondes' Captain liked the team to be focused on the game to come and not be chatting to girl friends or wives.

She did not know why she was so nervous and unsure of herself. She thought, '*Hopefully it is just the wounds and that I have not seen him for some time.*' She joined Ruth on the touchline. She told Polly the game had only been going for about ten minutes and as yet there had been no score. They were chatting away and Ruth was telling Polly her news, when, to her horror, Polly saw Dick charge down a kick and collapse on the ground. She showed a lot of restraint and did not run on to the pitch. The players were all around him and so she could not see what was going on. A spectator ran on with a bucket of water and a sponge. Polly wished she had thought of doing that.

Then Polly saw that two 'Nondes' players were virtually carrying Dick off the pitch. They were either side of him. He had his arms over their shoulders, but they were totally supporting him, with their arms around his waist. Polly could restrain herself no longer she ran to him as they reached the touchline. She said to one of the players who was supporting Dick,

"I will take him. You go back on the pitch."

"Are you strong enough?" Polly just remembered to smile,

"Of course I am I have been lifting oryx all week."

160

Another male spectator, who Polly did not know, took over from the second player who ran back on to the pitch. They carried Dick into the changing room. Polly could tell Dick did not know, where he was, nor did he recognise her. She turned to the other spectator and said,

"I'm Polly. I'm Dick's fiancé."

"I'm Reg. I used to play with Dick, but I'm too old now."

They laid Dick out on to one of the benches. Polly was terrified, as he just lay there. She felt his pulse which seemed to be going at his normal resting speed. She knew because most nights, when they slept together, she had her head on his chest and she would go to sleep listening to the rhythm of his heart. His eyes were staring up at her. One pupil was larger than the other. Polly knew enough first aid to know that was a bad sign. She turned to Reg.

"I wonder if we could find a doctor."

"Someone has gone to 'Parklands', as there are two doctors who play hockey for them." Polly knew that Parklands was really near, as she always parked her Landover there.

Suddenly Dick shook his head and sat up. He took in his surroundings and said,

"I must get back on the pitch. They will be one short." He went to get up, but Polly held him down.

"Just relax you have had a bad hit on the head. You should not go anywhere for a bit." Dick said,

"Don't boss me about Jean. You always think you know best." Polly tried to soothe him,

"Just take your time. They are doing fine on the pitch. Let me feel the back of your head."

"Don't fuss, Jean. I'm fine." He shook his head again. He screwed his eyes up. Polly guessed that he had a bad headache. She drew his head into her breasts and felt the back of his head. She found some blood in his hair and a lump about the size of a hen's egg. Polly was really worried. She was sure he had concussion. She thought, '*who the bloody hell is Jean? Whoever she was she certainly wasn't helping!*' Polly was at a loss to know how to stop him from going back on the pitch. Perhaps Reg would help.

"Reg, can you look at the wound on the back of Dick's head?" Dick was speaking, but Polly held his head, so tight to her breasts that all she could hear was him mumbling. Reg had a good look,

"He has got a deep cut and a swelling." Polly replied,

"That's what I thought. He also has one pupil larger than the other. I'm sure he has concussion. He definitely should not go back on the pitch." Dick could hear OK. He started to struggle. She held his head. He was very much stronger than her. He just stood up. She would not let go of his head and so he lifted her off the floor. He was frantic. He brought his hands round her back and ripped both sides of her dress. He yanked her arms away from his head. Polly could see he was about to wheel and rush out. She brought her knee up hard into his groin. He doubled over and vomited. At that moment one of the doctors from Parklands came in. He looked at Polly standing in her underwear. She looked at him and managed to smile,

"You won't believe this, but I'm his fiancé and I have just had to knee him in the balls to stop him running out on to the pitch to continue playing. He has had a blow to the back of his head. His left pupil is larger than his right. I hope you can reason with him." Dick was lying on the floor in the foetal position, groaning. The doctor said,

"I'm Graham Jones. I will certainly do what I can. I recognise you. You are Polly Cavendish. You were pointed out to me at the Muthaiga Ball."

"Well I'm glad you do recognise me, because Dick doesn't. Can you help me to get him comfortable?"

Between them they got Dick into a more comfortable position. Graham looked into his eyes,

"I can see what you mean. His pupils definitely are not the same size. You are correct; he definitely should not go back on the pitch. Kneeing him in the balls was a bit extreme. I will just listen to his heart and then I will look at his testicles." Polly replied,

"I feel really bad about hurting him. He is just so much stronger than me. I know how headstrong he is. If I had let him go, he would have run on to the pitch. It was all I could think of to do." Graham said,

"He certainly is in a bad way. He should not have lost consciousness again. A blow to the testicles would not do that. His

162

heart seems OK. Would you like to get dressed and go outside and I will examine his testicles."

"Oh don't worry about me. Dick has certainly trashed my dress. I have seen his testicles before. I can tell you, if I have done them any damage. Graham replied,

"Well it is not normal for me to examine a patient in this situation." Polly was about to get cross, but remembered to smile. She pretended that Graham was worried about her lack of clothes rather than the fact that Polly should not be looking at Dick in the nude, so she said,

"Let me just put on his shirt which he was going to wear after the game, to cover my underwear. His bag is just here." Graham thought, *'This young lady is not one to argue with.'*

He took off Dick's shorts and his jockstrap with Polly looking on. She said,

"Thank goodness they don't seem to be swollen or bruised. It is his head that I'm worried about. Would it be safe to move him? I have a mattress in the back of my Landrover. We could lay him on that. I could take him home. Mobia, his cook, will help me, when I get there."

"Don't worry I will come with you."

"That's really kind. Do you mind getting my Landrover? I feel a bit of an exhibitionist, dressed like this. The keys are under the driver's seat. It is the only blue Landrover I know, other than the Police vehicles. It's in Parkland's car Park, facing this way."

When Graham got back, Dick was still unconscious. Polly had put her dress on and then had put Dicks shirt over the top. They carried Dick out and layed him in the back of the Landrover on the mattress. Polly got in and cradled his head in her lap. Graham drove and Polly gave him directions.

Mobia saw Polly's Landrover and came out to greet her. He looked very worried, when Polly told him what had happened. She introduced Graham. It was much easier with three of them carrying him in. Mobia asked Polly in Kikuyu, whether she would be staying for supper. Polly said she would and then asked Graham if he would like to stay for an early supper. She was quite surprised that he said he would enjoy that.

Mobia left them to start making supper. Graham and Polly took off Dick's rugby kit and Polly found a kikoi. She asked, "Do you think the cut on his head needs stitching?"

"Yes I think it does. I have brought my stitching kit we could do it now."

It was when Graham was washing the wound, having shaved off some of Dick's hair that Dick came round. His first words were,

"However did I get home?" Polly answered

"You got kicked on your head during the game and Graham Jones who is a Doctor helped me to bring you home. I imagine you have got a bit of a headache." Dick reached up to the wound on his head.

"Only a dull ache, but someone must have kicked me in the balls. They are bloody sore."

"Sorry that was me. It was the only way I could stop you running on to the pitch and playing again. You were obviously concussed. You pupils were different sizes, but they are the same now. Now lie still. Graham is going to stitch you up."

Graham set about the task with confidence and skill. Polly held Dick's hand. He gripped it really hard, when the local was injected, but after that he was happy for Polly to stroke it. Polly asked Dick, if he would like some supper, but Graham advised against anything to eat, as he thought Dick would be likely to vomit. Dick was extremely thirsty. Graham allowed him to drink, but only little and often.

Mobia had supper ready and so Polly left Dick to relax and took Graham through to eat. Graham said,

"I think I know the reason for Dick's severe neurological signs. I think, from what the spectators told me that he came straight to the game, having been on safari for several days. I think he was dehydrated which always makes blows to the head worse. Thank goodness he is drinking now. I think he should have gone to hospital and been put on a drip, but I'm sure that he is over the worse and he has you to nurse him. You did well not letting him go back on the pitch, even if your measures were a little extreme."

"I just did not know what to do. It was my father who told me, if I ever had problems with a man that I was to knee my assailant in the balls. I don't think he imagined it would be my fiancé!"

"I hope you don't mind me asking, but how old are you?"

164

"I'm nineteen. Why do you ask?"

"I have never met a girl still in her teens who is so mature. Mind you, I have never met any girl dressed in bra and knickers' calmly looking after a violent man in the men's changing room in a rugby club." He raised his glass.

"Thank you for my supper and an extremely interesting afternoon and evening. I was very interested in the way you talked to Dick's cook. Were you conversing in Kikuyu?"

"Yes, I was. I really respect and like Mobia. I think the two of us must make Dick look after himself better." Polly thought it was wiser not to tell Graham that she probably ought to look after herself better. The last thing she wanted was for him to find out about the wounds on her bottom. He would then at best want to give her an anti-tetanus injection and at worse want to examine her bottom. She thought, *'I think I would rather show him my tent-peg scar?'*

Graham was obviously very astute and asked,

"Why are you smiling?" Polly went scarlet. She was about to lie and then thought, *'I like this guy and I'm sure Dick will. Why should I lie?'* She answered,

"I was thinking very naughty thoughts. About a year ago when I was on safari, I fell onto a tent post. It was a bad quite deep cut into my groin. I knew it needed stitching, but I did not think it was serious enough to call the flying doctor. I did not like the idea of a long trip to Nairobi from the Tanzania Border, so I got on the radio using the veterinary frequency to see if a vet at Aitong could stitch it for me. Dick, who I had known since I was eight, heard me on the radio and said he was nearby. He stitched it up. I was worried that you being a doctor might not approve." Graham laughed,

"Now he is your fiancé! Was that how you got together? It is lucky he is a vet. If he had been a doctor he might have been struck off. Becoming involved with your patients is strictly taboo."

"No, if I am honest it was much earlier. I think I fell in love with him, when I was eight." Graham's eyebrows shot up. Polly spoke quickly.

"Please don't think that Dick did anything improper. He certainly did not. It was just that he was very kind, when he put my pony to sleep. Father was away and I felt very sad and alone. Now let's stop talking about me. Are you married?"

"No I'm not and I haven't even got a girl friend. I have never met the right one."

"I won't try and match make, but I do have quite a few female pals so can I ask you to dinner sometime?"

"I would like that a lot."

No more was said, but Polly made sure that she took down his private phone number. Dick was sound asleep, when they checked on him. Graham said that was a good thing and that Polly was to ring him in the morning. Then Polly made sure that Mobia stayed within earshot, while she returned Graham to 'Parklands'.

She was soon back. Although it seemed late because of the drama, in reality it was quite early and Polly did not think Mobia minded. She suddenly felt dead-beat and so was delighted to strip off and to slip into bed with Dick who did not wake.

Dick woke soon after 2.00 am feeling extremely thirsty. He loved the feeling of Polly cuddled up behind him. He tried to get up without disturbing her, but she was instantly awake.

"Are you OK?"

"I'm fine. I was just a little thirsty." Polly jumped out of bed.

"I'll get you some water." She was soon back and knelt on the bed holding the pint glass for him.

"Now don't drink too quickly." Dick reached up with both hands. He used one hand to direct the glass. With his other hand he cupped her breast and very gently squeezed it.

"No hankie pankie, but that feels good." Once he had drunk his fill he lay back and Polly lay on top of him. His hands reached down to her bottom. Before he could ask Polly said,

"I have been in the wars. A young male oryx nailed me with his horns. I didn't even know he was behind me in the dark. We had captured his four ladies and he was not very happy about it."

"You poor girl! That lovely bottom, is it sore? Let me kiss it better?"

"No way, it is gross. It was very bloody at first. Then it became infected. Now it is horrible with big dark scabs. I have been worrying that you will find it repulsive."

"There is no part of you that I will ever find repulsive."

"You are so lovely. I don't deserve a wonderful man like you, particularly as I kneed you in the balls."

"They are not aching now."

"Would you like me to fondle them? However you must not get excited after a blow to the head." Dick laughed,

"That's a tall order. I only have to think about you to get excited."

"Well you mustn't!"

With that she reached down with her hand and started kissing his neck. She felt him getting aroused. She mentally sighed with relief. She would never have forgiven herself, if she had damaged him. She would not let him make love, even though she longed for him. Eventually they slept.

He was back to his normal self in the morning and insisted that he brought her to a climax. She let him enter her and come deep inside her, thinking that being frustrated would do him more harm than sexual release. They had a lovely quiet day together. She stayed for Sunday night and left when he went to work on Monday morning. She did not even try to stop him going to work.

She came back again on Monday night and was delighted that he was very cheerful and seemed completely back to normal. After supper, when she was sitting in his lap while they were drinking coffee, he said,

"I've decided to give up playing rugby."

"I hope you are not giving up just for me, as you know that is what I would like."

"No I feel that I am playing as well as I will ever play and I would rather give up now than, when I feel my game start to slip. I'm sure Graham was right that coming straight on to the pitch to play, dehydrated from a long hot drive, was barmy. Because I am away so much I don't get to training sessions. However the main reason is that I want to spend time with you. If I have got time off work I want to be with you."

Polly burst into tears and buried her face in his chest. He stroked her hair and added,

"Anyhow you need looking after. How is that lovely little bottom?"

She looked up at him.

"It is still disgusting. Oh Dick you are so kind. I love you with all my heart."

"You have no idea how much I love you. Let's get planning. When are we going to do the second lot of blood samples for the American shipment? How about starting next weekend? I'm sure the DVS will let me take it as work. He thinks the world of you."

"That would be marvellous. Let's go down on the train after work on Friday."

"That really is a good idea. Come on lets go to bed."

"That also is a good idea." Polly raced him to the bedroom. She stripped at speed and jumped into bed, calling come on slow coach. I want you right now! Somehow the danger of raised blood pressure for a patient who had suffered severe concussion was forgotten.

As expected the train journey down was good fun. At dinner they met two girls from England who were travelling in Kenya for six weeks. After Dick and Polly's experience with Ophelia they had been rather wary of this type of visitor to Kenya. However these two were Irish air hostesses working for Aer Lingus. They seemed good fun. So Polly invited them to the quarantine for supper on the following evening. Elizabeth was a brunette and Jo was a very sexy blond. Polly teased Dick, when she was lying on top of him on the top bunk.

"What did you think of Jo?"

"She seemed a nice girl."

"That my love was the understatement of the year. Did you find her attractive?"

"Not half as much as I find you." He stopped any further interrogation by kissing her passionately. He was rewarded by Polly rubbing herself against him and then pushing him inside her. As soon as she undulated her pelvis, he ejaculated with a deep sigh. Polly had a big smile on her face as she went to sleep.

Noah was at the station to meet them. The girls came with them to the quarantine station, so that they knew its location. Then Noah took them to their hotel.

They started blood testing immediately. They did the larger animals first, as they required the most strength. They knew they would get tired in the heat and so then blood testing the smaller antelope, would not be so taxing. The day went well so at 5.00 pm, Polly called a halt so everyone could relax before Gertrude called them all for supper. They were just sitting down when Elizabeth and

Jo arrived. They were both fairly pink from the sun, but they said that they had been careful and neither of them had got burnt. There was a lot of laughter over supper as the staff tried to teach them some Swahili.

They worked hard on Sunday. Polly managed to get hold of Chris so he came to supper. Although he was a little shy as always, Jo was such an extrovert, she managed to get him to open up. Polly loved people watching. She was sure that actually Chris found Elizabeth more attractive. Chris eventually plucked up enough courage to invite Elizabeth and Jo to stay at the Smith Mackenzie Mess. They were delighted, as the beach hotel where they were staying was eating into their holiday money. Chris was very helpful to Polly, as he said he could organise the shipment of the blood samples.

Polly and Dick left on the evening train on the Monday, happy that the precious samples would get to the USA. When they were cuddled on their bunk, Polly asked Dick,

"Do you think Chris will score with one of the girls?"

"I doubt it, because there are two of them. If he could find another guy to take on Elizabeth then he might score with Jo. She certainly was up for it." Polly laughed,

"I think he found Elizabeth more attractive."

"Really?"

"Because she was so outward going, I know you fancied Jo, but I don't think he did." Polly then giggled,

"Often girls who are quiet are more fun in bed." Dick added,

"I noticed you are always pretty quiet. That adds up. Roll on to your tummy." Polly could not stop laughing,

"Are you putting me to the test?"

"No, I'm just having a good look at my favourite bottom. I think you have been very lucky. You have only got tiny scars. They definitely need kissing."

Polly did not really have a chance to be delighted with this statement, as he then buried his face in her groin and then, his tongue and fingers had her gasping in ecstasy.

When they both were spent they cuddled together and became drowsy with the noise and motion of the train. Polly murmured,

"I have been meaning to ask you. Have you ever had a girl friend called Jean?" Dick yawned,

169

"Not that I can remember. Certainly I have never had a proper relationship with a girl called Jean. Why do you ask?"

"Oh Dick, you are so funny. What you mean is that you have never shagged a girl called Jean. I asked, as, when you were concussed and were fighting with me to go back on the pitch, you called me Jean. You told me not to be so bossy." Dick laughed.

"Jean was the only girl in my year at college. She was extremely bossy. I kept well away from her, as she was the Professor of Medicine's pet. She could do no wrong. She used to watch the college rugby games. I certainly did not ever want to shag her!" Polly giggled,

"Can I be bossy? Because I have my legs either side of your thigh, the motion of the train has really turned me on." She did not have to say anymore as Dick was kissing her passionately. Soon he was poised above her. He teased her. Polly was thrusting up to him and begging him to enter her. She gasped, when he obliged. They trust together and she cried out, when they both climaxed. Then they slept.

Although they were sad to be parted at the station the next day, they both had naughty grins on their faces.

Chapter 20

Polly and Dick do some socialising

Polly was pleased to get a letter from Rin to say that all her animals were well. Also that Rin thought that the lioness was pregnant. Then she asked if she could come and spend some time with Polly, as she had three weeks leave. Polly replied that it would be marvellous if she could come and stay with her in Kenya.

Polly took Hak with her, when she met her at Embakasi. It was quite an emotional meeting. Rin was given a warm welcome by the other seven Kenyans who had been to Japan. Rin was spellbound by the beautiful view of the Athi Plains from the ranch. That evening Polly took her on a game drive at teatime. Polly could see that Rin had jet lag, but she managed to keep her awake until 8.00 pm so hopefully she would then have a good night's sleep and not wake in the night. As it was Rin slept until lunchtime! They got on very well together. They had an afternoon shopping in Nairobi.

That evening Polly got a call from Jo asking if she and Elizabeth could visit, as they had been visiting friends upcountry, but still had two days left of their holiday. Polly knew that Dick was going to be home so she decided to have a dinner party. She rang Graham and asked him. He was very enthusiastic. So Polly suggested that he stayed the night. She then had a real houseful.

Of course it was not a problem, as Josiah was used to having hunting clients and he got Gideon to let two of the hunting staff help him. The party was a great success. In fact it was a bit of a riot and they were all fairly drunk, when they went to bed. When Polly and Dick were cuddled up together after making love, Polly asked him if he thought Graham had fancied any of the girls. Dick had chuckled and replied that he thought Graham was gobsmacked and was spoilt for choice.

In the morning Dick had to leave early to go to work. Polly got up to see him off and then did some paperwork. Eventually the others got up for a late breakfast. Polly joined them. Graham obviously did not feel too bad. He ate his breakfast rapidly and said that he ought to get back to his practice as he had only taken off the first part of the morning. Polly walked with him to his car. She could see that he wanted to ask her something. Finally he plucked up courage and said,

"If there was a chance I would enjoy meeting Rin again?" Polly smiled at him and said,

"I will see what I can arrange." She kissed him on the cheek before he drove off.

Polly soon got an excuse to help Graham with his request. After Polly and Rin had taken Elizabeth and Jo to Embakasi to fly back to Ireland, they went to Dick's house for supper. Mobia welcomed them. He said Dick had rung and said that they were to make themselves at home as he was going to be late as he had a very sick bull at the CAIS. Rather than wait for him Polly and Rin elected to walk over and see what he was up to. They put on waterproof overalls and wellington boots which were provided for visitors. The askari on the gate said that Dick was in the collecting building. They made their way there. Rin was quite excited, as she obviously loved veterinary work, but did not get a chance to see any cattle.

Dick was delighted to see them. He explained that this Ayrshire bull which he had just examined was very ill. It had a very high temperature. The blood and lymph slides which he had taken were negative for tick borne disease. As expected there was no evidence of trypanosomiasis, as there were no tsetse flies at this altitude. He could feel nothing abnormal on rectal examination and the bull's rumen seemed to have stopped moving. He had decided that he would do a left flank laparotomy in case the bull had a sharp foreign body in its reticulum.

He got Polly and Rind to help him. He gave the bull a small injection of a sedative and an analgesic, into the vein under the base of its tail. Then Joseph clipped a three foot square area on the bulls left flank. Dick was going to operate on the bull in the standing position. He was going to use a regional anaesthetic block, called a paravertebral. Rin handed him four long spinal needles which he placed carefully at intervals adjacent to the spine in the lumbar region, where Joseph had clipped. Then Polly and Rin had to load up four 20 ml syringes with local anaesthetic for him to inject deep into

172

the muscle running along the spine to block the roots of the nerves which supplied the flank.

Dick and Rin then scrubbed up so that their arms and hands were sterile. Polly had to open the sterilised packets of instruments very carefully, so that she did not touch any of them. The instruments were then layed out by Dick on a sterile cloth on a trolley. Polly was fascinated, as Dick started the surgery.

First he made a six inch skin incision on the left hand side below the spine and behind the ribs. He explained that it would be big enough for him to put his arm through. The bull did not move so obviously the regional anaesthetic had worked. The next incision was through the thick muscle layers. There seemed to Polly to be an awful lot of blood, but Dick and Rin seemed unconcerned, even when an artery sprayed Rin in the face. Attached to the underside of these thick muscles was a glistening white membrane. As Dick's scalpel cut it, there was a hiss of air. Dick layed down his instruments on the sterile tray cloth on the trolley and plunged his arm into the abdomen of the bull. Rin patiently waited with her hands clasped in front of her. Polly guessed that was to make sure that she did not touch anything which was not sterile. It looked slightly as if she was offering a prayer. Polly thought, '*with all this blood about a prayer would not come amiss!*'

Dick said, "I think I can feel the problem. The poor old chap has got an enormous abscess on his liver. No wonder he feels so ill. You have a feel Rin and I will get a tube ready to drain it." Polly was dying to have a feel, but she knew that she was not allowed too, as she was not sterile. As it was, she now had plenty to occupy her. She had to open a sterile pack with a long rubber tube which had a large bore needle attached to one end. Joseph had got a bucket. Dick inserted the needle and tube into the abdomen. He said Polly should get ready, as pus would come out, when it stabbed the abscess. Joseph held the bucket ready, as Polly held the end of the tube down into it. She was not prepared for the dreadful smell. She gagged, but managed not to be sick. There was so much pus that Joseph had to get another bucket.

When Dick and Rin were happy that there was no more pus, they removed the tube. Then Dick got Rin to suture the rumen to the body wall. When she had finished Dick made an incision into the rumen

173

and once again plunged his hand inside the bull, but this time into the rumen. Polly had to hold up buckets as he emptied out some of the contents so that he could thoroughly feel the inside of the rumen. He managed to find a three inch flat-head roofing nail which had caused the problem. He passed it to Joseph who said that it was likely to have been dropped into the hay, when they had been putting a roof over the feeding area for the bulls, to keep the sun off them. Dick said that the bull had been lucky that the nail had penetrated the liver and not the heart. He told Polly that the front of the reticulum was adjacent to the diaphragm and there was very short distance to the pericardium which was the outside skin of the heart.

The hole in the side of the bull was soon sewn up. Polly was glad to get out into the fresh air. When they got back to Dick's house they all had showers, but she could not seem to get the smell of the revolting pus off her hands. Mercifully that did not stop her having a good supper.

Dick told Polly and Rin that he had to go on Safari up to the romantic island on the north Kenyan coast called Lamu. He said it would be a rough journey getting up there, but he wondered if they wanted to come. The two girls jumped at the idea. Polly had an idea. She would ask Graham. She kept the idea to herself. Polly and Rin stayed at Dick's house for the night. Mobia made them breakfast. They left at the same time as Dick went to work. On the way back to the ranch, Polly asked Rin if she thought it might be a good idea to ask Graham to come with them to Lamu. Rin had a smile on her face, when she nodded. When Polly rang Graham, he said he would love to come.

Chapter 21

A trip to Lamu

They set off early from Polly's house as that was south of Nairobi and their first destination was Mombasa. They were in Dick's Landrover so that he could claim mileage, as it was a Government safari, but he could take three passengers without any questions being asked.

They managed to get to Mtito Andei for breakfast. They were now in the middle of Tsavo Park. They all loved the big herds of elephant that they had seen. Initially it had been quite a squash as they all sat in the front of the Landrover, but now that it was hot, Dick took off both the tops of the doors to let more air in. They got very dusty, when other vehicles came in the opposite direction, as they were not on tarmac. The girls had stripped off to their bikinis. Polly, who was sitting between the gear stick and Dick's leg, loved the feel of Dick's thigh and even more the feel of his hand as it rested on her thigh. She had difficulty not to smile as she saw Graham's hand drop on to Rin's thigh. Rin did not push it away.

They got through Mombasa and up to Kilifi Creek. They stopped south of the creek at The Mnarani Club for a late lunch. Dick smiled after lunch as his three passengers all dozed off to sleep, when they had crossed Kilifi Ferry. They ended up camping in Tana River District north of the Sabaki River. They managed to find some Kapok trees which gave them some nice shade. Dick rigged up the shower behind a Baobab tree. He strung a washing line up so that the towels, not only could dry, but also to give Rin and Polly some privacy. They washed all the clothes as they were all filthy from the dust. They had bought some fresh meat, vegetables and fruit in Malindi, so supper was a feast. They enjoyed their coffee laced with 'Amarula' in the moonlight, as the fire was only glowing after being used to heat the water and to cook the food. Dick had turned off the gas light.

Polly was dying to know how the sleeping arrangements were going to work out. They had not brought beds, but two mattresses. There were no mosquitoes, but it was very hot. Polly, Dick and Graham slept in kikois. Rind wrapped herself in a very pretty length of silk. There was some laughter about snoring. The boys had to sleep on the outside and the girls on the inside of their make-shift dormitory on the ground. Poly pushed Dick on to his back and lay on top of him, as she normally did. She noticed that Rin cuddled Graham's back.

They were all awake with the dawn. Dick managed to revive the fire to boil the kettle for tea and cook some breakfast. The four of them soon packed up the camp. They reached the ferry at Garsen at mid-morning, only to find that it was not working because the Tana River had burst its banks again and the whole area was flooded. Daniel Toya, the head veterinary scout and the rest of the veterinary staff came to rescue. They commandeered some canoes to cross the river. They said that if they would walk two miles on the other side, there were Landrovers which could carry them to Mkowe.

They carried as little luggage as they could manage with, for two nights. The girls stripped down to their bikinis and the guys held the canoe for them to get in. Rin sat down in the canoe and then with a squeak she jumped up. Under some old wet rags was a catfish which the owner of the canoe had caught for his dinner. Its long spiky tentacles had tickled her thighs and frightened Rin, but when she saw what it was she laughed,

"Can we have fish for supper tonight, Dick? In Japan we eat a lot of fish and I miss it. In Japan we do not allow fish to tickle girl's bottoms." Dick answered,

"I think you will be lucky for most of your meals in Lamu. Fish and seafood is about all they eat. I promise you I won't tickle your bottom." Polly thought, '*I bet Graham would like to do that!*"

In fact it was lucky that the two girls were brave, as there were several crocodiles and a large number of hippos visible from the canoes, as they crossed the river. Daniel Toya volunteered to send some of his men over the river, but Dick told him they could easily manage for two miles. Even so it was a very hot walk. Polly was glad they had brought plenty of water.

Dick knew one of the owners of a Landrover. He was called Sayd Budjra. He was happy to give them a lift to Mkowe. On the way he insisted that they stopped at his home in Witu, as his father would be upset if he did not see Dick. Polly knew the Arab family would be Moslems. She asked Sayd, if she and Rin should wait in the Landrover. Sayd said it would be quite OK, if they wrapped a kikoi around their bodies and covered their heads and shoulders. He said he was sure his father would actually love to see a girl in a bikini, but his father would have to pretend that he would be shocked.

In fact the old man was a kindly person and greeted the girls warmly and thanked them for respecting their customs. They took their shoes off and were ushered into the cool house. They were given sweet tea, cold lemon juice and cakes which tasted of cashew nuts. Polly was worried that their dirty feet would spoil the beautiful carpets, but the old man said that they were not to worry. He said he was so pleased to see Dick who had always helped him with his cattle. He was amazed, when Polly explained to him in Swahili that Rin was also a vet. He bowed his head in reverence.

Sayd then took them to Mkowe, where the staff gave Dick a big welcome. They were taken in the veterinary boat to Lamu Island. Graham, Polly and Rin were fascinated by The Arab Town of Lamu which had a lot of Portuguese influence. They went to the veterinary office where they met the cheerful, Indian, District Livestock Officer (DLO) Suleiman. He offered them tea and some very fiery Samosas. Rin laughed and said she thought they must have been made in Korea because they were so hot. The inside of the veterinary office was quite cool, as it had a high ceiling.

They made a plan for the morning. Dick's visit had been arranged over the radio some days ago. There had been sick animals in two of the three groups' villagers cattle. They had been showing respiratory signs. Some had died. In the morning they were going to blood test all the sick animals and the same number of healthy animals. Also if an animal had died they were going to do a Post Mortem (PM).

On the seaward side of Lamu Island there are beautiful beaches. The town, where they were, was on the landward side. There was an interesting water front. They had only to walk a few yards north to come to the only hotel on the island, called Petley's Inn. It was fairly basic accommodation, but they commandeered two rooms. The girls thought the upstairs long-drop was rather revolting. Water was brought up to their rooms in large jugs. They had a big china bowl in their rooms to wash in. Dick told them that the water on Lamu was good. It came from wells. The legend was that the water came under ground and under the sea from the Ewaso Ng'iro River. This was the same river which Polly had crossed a few weeks ago at Barsalinga before they had captured the oryx. This river disappeared into the Lorien Swamp in the NFD and never reappeared and hence the legend.

As Polly had seen Rin cuddle up to Graham on the previous night she did not worry that Rin was sharing a room with Graham. They both seemed happy with the arrangement.

As there was still two hours of daylight left they decided to go for a walk northwards. Dick said that it was easier to get to a good beach that way. He said if they tried to walk eastwards across the island it was easy to get lost in the sand dunes and that the bush was quite thick. The path took them to the end of the town and then along the sea shore which was covered in seaweed. They came to a very small fishing village, called Shella which was on the northern most point of the island. From then on eastwards there were the most glorious beaches backed by coconut palms. It was a very beautiful romantic setting. They all had a swim. Polly and Dick sat together under the palms. Graham and Rin walked hand in hand further along the beach. Polly had whispered to Dick that they should leave them to be on their own.

After about half an hour, Polly and Dick went in for another swim. Initially the sand went out so that the water came up to Polly's bikini top. The water was really very warm. It was only when the sand dropped away and they could not stand that it got cooler. They had a good swim and then as they came into the shallower water, Polly wrapped her arms around his neck and her legs round his waist. They kissed. Polly loved the feel of him hard against her. When they stopped kissing Polly said,

"It is good fun travelling with other people, but I do value are time alone together. I really want to make love to you, but I know it won't be very satisfying in the water and I would be too embarrassed under those palm trees in case we get caught by the others. I love you so much Dick."

178

"I love you too. You are so gorgeous. I love just hugging you and I love looking at you. You have the most beautiful body." Polly laughed,

"Even with the scars on my bottom?" It was Dick's turn to laugh,

"They make you unique. I bet there is no other girl in the world that has identical scars on her bottom which were caused by an Oryx."

"You may be right about that. I will never know why I was not shy in that room in Soy Country Club. I was a real tart I just stood naked in front of you and turned round to show you the scar in my groin. It is frightening really, one's sex drive. I might have understood it if I was drunk, but I think I was sober. You were certainly sober, when you kissed my fanny after you had stitched me up. It was so out of character for you to be so bold." Dick chuckled,

"It might have been something that I would later have really regretted. It might have terrified you."

"Well luckily it only surprised me. Every time I pull up a pair of knickers I see the scar and think of you." They kissed again and then walked up through the surf holding hands. They found Graham and Rin sitting holding hands under a palm tree. They set off to walk back to the town.

They were all very hot and sticky, when they got to the hotel. Dick found some buckets so they washed off the worst of the sand and salt in a deserted little garden next to the hotel. In their room Polly and Dick took off their swimming things and sponged each other using the big bowl and the jug of water. It was very refreshing. Polly said,

"I wonder how Rin and Graham are getting on." Dick said,

"If they have any sense they will have done the same." Polly looked pensive. She thought that they might be too shy. When they met for supper she realised she had been wrong. It was not difficult to tell that Graham and Rin were now an item. They all, particularly Rin enjoyed the fish curry. They were not late to bed. They had ordered breakfast for 6.00 am as they wanted to start testing the cattle early in the morning.

It was hot work. Dick had to do a PM at the second village. The others all watched. Flies were everywhere. Luckily the villagers found them plenty of water to wash off any blood. Dick was very gloomy, as he knew without taking the samples that he was dealing with an outbreak of Contagious Bovine Pleural Pneumonia (CBPP). Rin had heard of the disease, when she was at veterinary college, but she had never seen a case, as Japan is totally free of the condition. Dick explained that it was a disease caused by strange bacteria which were unusual because they did not have solid cell walls. It only occurred in cattle, but there was a similar condition, but caused by a different bacteria, in goats. Polly asked,

"What will happen now?" Dick answered,

"I'm not sure. The disease occurs in Masailand and in isolated places in the NFD. We try to control it by limiting the movement of cattle unless they have been blood tested and found to be free of the disease." Graham asked,

"Is there a vaccine?" Dick replied,

"There is, but it is pretty primitive. It does confer immunity, but it causes a very nasty reaction in a lot of cattle. We have to inject it into their tails and often their tails drop off. As you can imagine the Masai don't like that, and so they don't tend to bring their cattle forward." Polly said,

"Poor cows." Dick added,

"Life is hard. Having the disease and having a lingering death must be horrible. I think the best thing would be to slaughter all the cattle on Lamu Island and supply the islanders with clean blood tested cattle. That's what I will recommend." Rin said,

"I expect that will mean that you will have to visit Lamu lots of times. I hope you will bring us it is such a magically place." Polly guessed then that Rin and Graham had got on rather well last night! That evening Polly was like a mother hen making them get to bed early as she knew the return journey was going to be very tiring on the following day.

Although it was tiring it had its highlights. As they were getting into the canoe, Graham tickled Rin's bottom pretending to be a catfish. She jumped up nearly capsizing the canoe and then wrapped her arms around him, kissing him. The whole incident caused a lot of laughter. When they camped on the way home, Graham put their mattress quite a distance from Polly and Dick's. Polly was sure they made love very quietly. She and Dick did the same!

When they got back to the ranch, Rin and Graham shared a room and in the morning Rin asked Polly, if she minded if she went to stay with Graham. Polly kissed Rin and said that she was really pleased for her and that she hoped everything would work out for them.

Polly got up early with Dick to see him off to work. She then started to tackle her mail. There was good news. The second lot of blood samples taken from the American shipment had passed. Now Polly had to get the animals shipped to the States. She was keen to get them off as soon as possible. The FMD situation in Kenya was constantly changing. The sooner they were at sea the better. She booked a telephone call to Chris in Mombasa. She expected a delay, but was surprised, when she got through in twenty minutes. He already knew all the details regarding the size and destination of the shipment. He promised he would get shipping for her as soon as possible. She trusted him. She might not have trusted Roger. She wondered how he was getting on in Mwanza. She hoped that he hadn't taken to drink which was always a danger for young men in fairly remote postings. She asked Chris to do her a favour and get word to the PVO Coast Province, as he would have to have an input. Chris said that was no problem, as he could put through a local call.

In fact it did not take long for Chris to arrange shipping and so Polly, Gideon and the team moved down to Mombasa in the lorry. They left Hak with Noah and the Landrover in case there was a drama at the ranch. Polly and Gideon had already agreed that it was his turn to take a trip. Polly could tell he was quite excited. Eight different guys also were going to go, to make it fair. Polly just hoped that they all would not be seasick. She had a chat with Graham and he advised that they took tablets. He said they made some people drowsy, but as no one would be driving or working heavy equipment that would not be a problem. He also told Polly that he had booked up a holiday in Japan. He said,

"I owe you, a big thank you." Polly replied,

"I'm really happy for you both."

Now that they knew the form the loading went very well. When they were alone together during the loading Polly teased Chris asking him, if he wasn't going to ask her out on a bum-boat in the harbour for a drink and a swim. He replied that it had certainly been a novel way to sober up quickly. Polly also asked him to arrange a boat to take her and Dick together with the Oryx to Bahrain. He said he would be delighted to, as the more work he got the better were his promotion prospects.

Polly and the staff who were remaining in Kenya stayed at the docks to wave them off. Then they returned to the ranch to organise the Oryx to come down to Mombasa. This was straight forward as they could come down on the lorry. Polly timed it so that they arrived on the right day to be loaded immediately so that they had as little stress as possible. The Bahrain authorities did not require them to be quarantined.

Dick left his arrival down in Mombasa to the last minute so as to use as little of his local leave as possible. Polly thought something dreadful had happened to him, as he was not on the dock, when the boat was due to sail. The Captain would not wait. Even Polly's smile would not make him delay. To her relief Dick came out on the boat which came to take off the pilot at the mouth of the harbour. She was so pleased to see him that she couldn't be cross. She just whispered into his ear. I think I am sleeping on my own on the top bunk for the whole voyage! She knew very well that their cabin had a double bed. She tried to look cross, but her giggle gave her away. They were still in sight of land, when Dick had got all her clothes off and was tickling her until she begged for mercy.

It was on the second morning after they had finished feeding and were having breakfast that Dick casually said,

"Have you got anything planned for today?"

"No why do you ask?"

"I have been speaking to the Captain and he said he would be happy to marry us."

A broad grin came on her face, when she realised that he was serious.

"Richard Brendon. What a marvellous idea. I will get married in my bikini! I wonder what Auntie Margaret will have to say about that!"

#0114 - 011217 - C0 - 210/148/10 - PB - DID2050740